BATTLE
GROUND

RACHEL CHURCHER

Zoe,
Time to be brave..."

Battle Ground (Battle Ground #1)

First published by Taller Books, 2019

ISBN 9781096670957

Cover design by Medina Karic:
www.fiverr.com/milandra

WWW.TALLERBOOKS.COM

Notes

Margie's name is pronounced with a hard 'g', like the 'g' in Margaret: Marg-ie, not Marj-ie.

Leominster is a town in Herefordshire, UK. It is pronounced 'Lem-ster'.

BEX

AUGUST

Prologue

Silence. Darkness. My pulse, loud in my ears.

We're under attack.

We need to move. We need to get out. Three floors underground in a nuclear bunker – we're safe while no one knows we're here, but if they've found us, we're trapped. One way in, and one way out.

Voices. Sounds. Hammer blows, slamming through the silence.

I force myself to wake up. Open my eyes, push back the blanket, crawl out of bed.

I need to wake the others.

Boots. Armour. Gun.

Time to be brave.

BEX

JUNE

(TWO MONTHS EARLIER)

Marching

We've been marching for days. We've slept in school halls, in sports halls, in community centres. Everywhere, people have been kind. We've had hot food and blankets, and neighbours have come to thank us for signing up. We've even had gifts: clothing, food, small luxuries. No one seems quite sure how to treat us, but they are grateful, so they do their best.

But we didn't sign up. We're conscripted troops. We didn't get a choice. They've started doing that now, in the places where they don't get enough volunteers.

We thought about signing up. We talked about it – Dan and Margie and me in our boarding school library. We'd stay late, after private study and play cards for chocolate, talking. The pay was good, the risks were low, and you'd come out at the end with training and experience. You'd be protecting the people: teachers, doctors, nurses, and everyone else from terrorist attacks and terrorist bombs. The real army would do the proper fighting – we would just be the visible deterrent, the school guards, the hospital security. Keeping the terrorists away from people who wanted to go to work and come home again, safe from the threat of attack.

But we wanted to *be* the doctors, the teachers, the leaders. Dan and I, we chose to stay at school.

Margie took a different path. She'd been wondering about the terrorists, about what made them fight. She spent time with Dr Richards, our History teacher, working through the causes of the conflict, figuring out what each side was trying to achieve. She said less and less during our card games, and then one day, she wasn't there at all.

She didn't show at breakfast, or at the first lesson. I went to her dormitory between classes, and found her books and her tablet stacked neatly on her desk, uniform laid out on the bed, and half her belongings tidy in the cupboard. The other half was gone, along with her rucksack, boots and winter coat. I sat on her bed, feeling as if someone had drained the air from the room. I hadn't imagined that she would leave. Or that Dr Richards would leave with her, to join the terrorists.

*****

We're marching again. I'm carrying my clothes and a few possessions in a rucksack on my back. My walking boots are dirty, and I'm wearing the same trousers and T-shirt that I wore yesterday. We don't stop anywhere for long enough to wash our clothes, but sometimes local people take in laundry for us, and return it in the morning, neatly folded, before we start another day of marching.

We're trying to guess where they're taking us, but no one's telling us the plan. There are rumours: we're going to London to guard the government; we're going to Harwich to guard the port; we're just marching, so people can see the brave volunteers and start to feel safe again.

Our recruiters give us daily briefings, after breakfast, but they don't tell us anything useful – just how long each day's march will be, and whether anyone is on report for misbehaving. Discipline means carrying the recruiters' rucksacks as well as your own. It's not a good idea to misbehave.

We're all lined up in last night's sports hall, rucksacks at our feet, waiting for today's briefing. There's a blister on my left foot, so I'm trying to shift my weight onto my right foot while standing to attention. Everything hurts, and I want to stop marching. I think of my books, on my desk at school, and I wish that all I had to worry about was an essay deadline or busy day of lessons.

The recruiters are standing around outside the hall, making us wait. I can hear their conversation through the open door. The sound of a vehicle makes them fall silent, and they line up, waiting for someone. A battered 4x4 pulls up in the car park, and a tall man in camouflage battle fatigues gets out, followed by a shorter man in a neat uniform. The tall man salutes the recruiters, and gestures to them to enter ahead of him.

The recruiters march into the hall, followed by the two men. The shorter man holds a clipboard and a pen, and stands, ready to take notes. The tall man has high, chiselled cheekbones, an almost superhero-style square jaw, and a muscular build. He stands in front of us and looks us up and down.

"Recruits!" he bellows.

"Sir!"

"I am Commander Bracken of the Recruit Training Service, and thanks to the Emergency Armed Forces Act, you are now under my command. By the end of today, you'll be at RTS Camp Bishop, where you will stay and undergo training. I don't want to hear complaints, I don't want to hear problems. I want to hear solutions and answers. If there's a problem, get it sorted. If you're tired, get some sleep. If you're aching, keep moving. If you're hungry, go for a run. Be self-sufficient, and we'll get along fine."

He turns to the recruiters.

"Any troublemakers I should know about?"

"No, Sir!"

The shorter man makes a note on his clipboard.

"At ease, recruits. See you at Camp Bishop this evening."

The Commander turns on his heel, says a few quiet words to the recruiters, and heads back out to the car.

The shorter man follows. As they drive away, the recruiters are shouting at us to get moving, get our packs on, get lined up, and out of the door. Another day's march begins.

Arrival

We stop for lunch – a meal of soup and bread, provided by kind people in a church hall on a high-rise housing estate – and I bribe another recruit with a can of drink from my pack to switch places with me so I can march next to Dan. We keep up the brisk pace in silence until we're out of town, and walking along a busy road. The cars driving past sound their horns as they pass us, acknowledgement of our service.

"What do you think? Sleeping in the same place for more than a night?"

Dan grins. "Sounds good to me."

"And training. Finally. Do you think they'll tell us what we're here for?"

"Nah. They're going to keep us in the dark. Train us up, and then keep us on call for when the bad guys start something."

The bad guys. Margie and Dr Richards. Everything seems very real, suddenly. We've got so used to marching and sleeping, marching and sleeping – I haven't been thinking about what happens when we get to where we're going. That we're going to be fighting our best friend.

There's an ache in my chest. I don't ever want to be fighting Margie.

Dan sees the look on my face, and hurries to change the subject. "What about Batman and Robin?"

I look at him, blank-faced.

"The commander, and his clipboard man. Commander Square Jaw and his sidekick? Batman and Robin!"

And we're laughing, even though I can't bear to think about what happens next.

*****

We make it to Camp Bishop in the evening. It's a field, surrounded by woodland, with temporary modular buildings for dormitory blocks. Two Senior Recruits in uniform are waiting for us a mile from the camp, and they parade us along the Leominster bypass, where people driving home from work will notice our arrival. The bypass runs past the western side of the camp, and we approach the front gate along a narrow lane, lined with trees, that curves away out of sight on the far side. I can see the lights of the town and the streetlights from the bypass as we turn into the camp entrance, past a tall wire fence, a guardhouse, and a line of vehicles painted in olive green and camouflage.

I'm tired and hungry, and the blister on my foot is hurting. As we walk through the gates, we can smell the evening meal being prepared, and it is torture to have to line up, listen to a briefing, and follow the camp staff to our assigned rooms. I'm sharing with five other girls, most of whom joined us on the march. We introduce ourselves quickly – we're all exhausted and hungry. I drop my pack on my bunk, haul out the sweatshirt I packed at the top, and head back to the dining room.

Dan is there ahead of me, his smart shirt crumpled and dirty and his hair untamed. We stand in line for bowls of meat stew and mashed potatoes. It smells amazing, and I'm so hungry when we sit down to eat that I don't think I taste it at all. We don't speak until our bowls are clean. It's so good to be full, and sleep in a real bed, and to have finished our long march.

We're just commenting on how happy we are to be here, when Commander Bracken walks in with his side-kick. Batman and Robin. Dan grins at me, and I grin back.

There is an ear-grating sound as everyone pushes their chairs back at once to stand to attention.

"Recruits!"

"Sir!"

"At ease." I gratefully take the weight off my blistered foot.

"Welcome to RTS Camp Bishop, Unit 77B! You can sit down." The noise of all the chairs moving again silences the Commander. He looks around the room, appraising us as we sit. I look at the people around me. Dirty faces, dirty hair, dirty clothes. I'm pretty sure the first order of business is cleaning ourselves up and getting ourselves looking smart again.

I'm right.

"You've seen your dorms, you've seen your beds. There are showers, there are laundry rooms. By tomorrow morning, I expect to see all of you cleaned up, sweet-smelling, and presentable. Breakfast is at six-thirty."

A murmur builds around the room, and drops away as the commander continues.

"On your way out of this hall, you will collect your Recruit Training Service uniforms." The camp staff are filing into the space next to the door, setting up long tables, and carrying in bundles of clothing. "Take care of your uniforms. Keep them clean and smart. Problems are to be addressed to the camp manager."

"Things I do not wish to see: dirty uniforms; torn uniforms; damaged uniforms; disrespected uniforms. You are responsible for cleaning, fixing, and protecting your uniforms. Outside this camp, you are on show. The public trusts you to protect them, to be professional. This starts with looking smart and demonstrating your capability to look after yourselves."

I'm exhausted, and I've had a good meal. All my muscles ache. It's all I can do to stay awake while the commander talks. I'm fighting to keep my eyelids open, when, at another table, someone's chin drops to their chest, and they begin to snore.

We all understand, and we all know that could have been any of us. The commander pauses, and nods to Robin. His assistant strides over to the sleeping recruit, and slams his clipboard down onto the table in front of him.

"Name!" He shouts, into the boy's face. He's awake, now, and terrified.

"Saunders, Sir!" He's slurring his words. He's sitting up straight and giving his head quick shakes to wake himself up properly.

"Mister Saunders. Do you think it is respectful to sleep while the commander is talking?"

Saunders shakes his head. "No, Sir. Sorry, Sir."

Robin steps back, and the commander continues.

"Recruits!"

"Sir!"

"Stand!" The chairs scrape against the floor again.

"Camp staff will call out your names. When you hear your name, walk to the table, collect your uniform, take it back to your dorm, and check it. Any problems, bring it back. The camp manager will be here to make exchanges and make sure you have what you need. Saunders!"

"Sir!"

"You will stand where you are until the other recruits have their uniforms. When the last of your colleagues has left, then you may collect your uniform."

"Yes, Sir."

Saunders' voice shakes as he responds. As we wait for our names to be called, I see him clenching his fists, and pinching his leg, struggling to stay awake. I can't help sympathising – that could so easily have been me.

The camp staff are calling out names, alphabetically. I'm up quickly, and I give Dan a nod as I leave. I take the bundle of clothing with my name on, scribble a signature on the list of recruits, and head back to the dorm.

We discussed it, of course, while we played cards and enjoyed our library privileges. Dan didn't like the loss of our rights, but he thought the government was doing the right thing, hiring new soldiers and making new laws to fight the terrorists. We'd beat them more quickly this way, and life would go back to normal. Margie was angry, and couldn't talk to Dan without shouting. She could see our rights being taken away, but she couldn't see a path to bringing them back. She was sure we were selling our democracy and our freedom in exchange for safety that the government couldn't give.

I listened to them both, and I struggled to decide. Fighting the terrorists was a good thing. Soldiers on the street to keep us safe had to be a good thing. The cost wasn't too high if it saved lives, was it?

I didn't think it would affect us like this. Margie's disappearance. Our conscription. Our rights to finish our education, to make decisions about our own lives – those had been taken away, and we hadn't even noticed.

And the bombings didn't stop. If anything, the bombers became more brave, more destructive, more daring. They seemed to be everywhere. Attacks became more frequent, and the government used this as an excuse to hold onto power. The more the terrorists attacked, the less power remained with the people. We had signed away our freedoms for empty promises of protection.

So they passed the Emergency Armed Forces Act, and they came to school. They took the registers and the student records. They called everyone who'd turned 16, lined us up, told us what to wear and what to bring, and they started us on our long march. More recruits joined the group as we marched, conscripted from other schools. The recruiters told us that we were the new

front line in the defence of civilian life, and they thanked
us for our service.

Caring

The morning is a mad rush. Most of us went straight to sleep after checking our uniforms, so the showers are packed before breakfast, and we're all elbowing each other out of the way to get to the basins and the mirrors – no one wants to draw the attention of Batman and Robin this morning.

I get cleaned up, wash and brush my hair, and get dressed in my new, freshly pressed uniform. Camouflage and khaki with an RTS patch on the sleeve – nothing unexpected, but it takes away our individuality. It makes me feel awkward, and less like myself, but at the same time there is safety in blending into the group.

We're unrecognisable as we line up for trays of hot food. We're not the dishevelled marchers who sat here last night. We look like a fighting force, the protectors of the people, the defenders against terror. I keep looking around, trying to recognise the people I have come to know over our days of marching.

But there are more recruits with us this morning. People who have been here for longer, who arrived before we did. There are other dorms, and other teams with more training and more experience of the camp. We're going to have to work doubly hard to avoid the commander's notice.

I sit next to Dan, both of us smart and clean in our new uniforms. Dan's even brushed his hair, but that's not enough to tame it completely, and I can't help smiling at his rolled-up sleeves. He's exchanged a civilian shirt for a uniform, but they look the same on him. He looks as if this is what he aways wears – he's completely at home and comfortable in the starchy fabric.

Saunders walks past our table, dragging his feet and yawning, and looking as if he hasn't slept. His dark hair is a mess, and his bootlaces are untied. Dan and I beckon him over and he sits down next to us, propping his chin on his hand and staring at his breakfast.

"Bex", I say, offering him my hand, "and this is Dan."

He mumbles a greeting, shakes my hand, and looks as if he might fall asleep again. After last night, he can't afford to make another mistake.

I give him a smile.

"Get some coffee into you. You'll feel better."

He nods, vaguely, and reaches for his cup. I pour coffee for him from the insulated jug on the table, and he drinks, grimacing. We haven't spoken before, during the march. I think he joined a day later than we did, but I can't recall. If he's here, he must be at least sixteen, but his small frame makes him seem fragile, and he looks a lot younger. An easy target for the Senior Recruits, if they're anything like the recruiters.

We eat in comfortable silence, refilling the coffee cups as soon as they start to look empty.

*****

I've been a carer all my life. Mum was injured in a car accident when I was a few months old, and looking after her became the glue that held our family together. Dad worked wonders when I was too young to help out, and when I graduated from riding on Mum's lap in her wheelchair to walking with Dad, all I wanted to do was grow tall enough to push her myself. Dad was in charge of the wheelchair, and it was my job to make sure we had all the bags, medication, and equipment we needed for our days out. We made an amazing team, and I loved having such a responsible job to do.

But then Dad got sick, and for a while I was looking after both of them. I was missing days of school, and my priority in life was making sure their needs were met.

Mum was so proud of me for juggling their care with living my own life, but when my grades started to slip, and Mum and Dad needed more care, she was the one who suggested boarding school.

I was torn. I didn't want to leave them, but I wanted to concentrate on my education. I was so used to being on call 24 hours a day, I couldn't imagine someone else taking care of them instead of me. But then Dad got worse, and Mum insisted that they move into a care home. She and I made all the arrangements together. We sold the house, and we found them somewhere to live where they would be happy and have carers and doctors on call when they needed them.

On the day the house was sold, I stood on the pavement outside, surrounded by my bags and boxes. A neighbour had driven us all to the care home, where I'd helped my parents to settle in, and said a tearful goodbye. Mum kept smiling, gave me a massive hug and told me she was proud of me. I knew I would be back to visit them, but I would never live with them again.

The neighbour drove me home, and helped me carry the last of my belongings out of the house. We called a taxi, and locked the door for the last time. I waited on the pavement, suddenly understanding that I was leaving, and that I wasn't coming back. The taxi arrived, and the neighbour helped to pack my things into the boot. It looked like such a small amount of stuff to be taking to my new home, and that's when I started to cry. The neighbour gathered me up in a huge hug, and told me that I'd be OK. That everything would work out. And she promised to visit my parents and make sure they were happy.

I climbed into the taxi, and set off for my new life. My home dropped back, out of sight, and my neighbour stood waving until we turned the corner. I dried my tears, and tried to think about the good things this would *bring. I would be able to give my full attention to my education. I would be able to go to university, and get a job where I could help people. Maybe a doctor or a teacher.*

I was fourteen years old.

Introduction

Day one is harder than any of us imagined.

The commander briefs us on our duties and on the training plan. As new recruits, we begin with a cross-country run. Out of the base, across the bypass where two Senior Recruits stop the traffic for us, over the railway bridge, and along the main road into town. Through an industrial estate and back across the bypass, returning through the woods and circling the camp's outer fence until we're back at the gate. Once again, I think they're showing us off. Letting the public see the recruits who will keep them safe from the terrorists.

As we run through the gates, camp staff hand us bottles of water from stacks of crates, and we run past the dorms to the training field. Five minutes to drink up and fall into ordered lines. Then weapons training.

I've never held a gun, and looking at my fellow recruits, I don't think many of them have, either. A Senior Recruit called Ketty runs the training. She swaggers out in front of us, holding up a futuristic-looking rifle.

"Can anyone tell me what this is?" She barks.

We're all still catching our breath from the run. We all stand, silent, hoping that she doesn't pick on us.

"Come on. Anybody."

I stand completely still, ignoring the blister on my foot, hoping that I'm not the one she'll pick on. She looks along the lines of recruits, and strides over to someone in the front row.

"Saunders! Mr Sleepy himself. Can you tell me what this is?" She's shouting, right in his face.

"A gun, Sir", he replies, quietly.

"Louder, Saunders!"

He pauses, takes a breath, and shouts, "A gun, Sir!"

"Thank you, Saunders." Ketty begins to pace up and down the space in front of us. "This is a gun. But this is not any gun. This is a prototype next-gen power-assisted rifle, firing armour-piercing bullets. Under normal conditions, you lot wouldn't get to see one of these until you'd been training for years, if ever. You'd have to pass tests, and show that you're big enough to use one of these. But these aren't normal circumstances. This is war, and this is war on our home territory, and the decision makers have decided to let you worms loose with their favourite toys. You'll be starting off with training bullets. We'll see how good you are, and whether you deserve to progress to armour-piercing rounds. Don't be fooled – training bullets will still kill you, so don't be stupid."

I concentrate on staring straight ahead. I've never been spoken to like this before, and Ketty is clearly enjoying the effect her speech is having on us.

"Make no mistake. You are getting your paws on these because the government wants to see them in use. The people in charge, they want you out there, waving these around to show Joe Public that we're protecting him. This isn't about you. This is about public confidence. About stopping panic and protecting people from themselves. While they can see you, and your guns, they'll be happy to get on with their lives and leave us to get on with ours.

"You are not fighting this war. We have a real army for that. You are showing the people that the war is being fought. You are the government's action figures. The front-line dolls. And public-facing dolls get the best weapons."

Front-line dolls. Not people. Not individuals. I glance at the recruits around me, our matching uniforms turning us into clones. No one cares about what happens to us, as long as the people out there feel safe.

Ketty stops pacing and turns to face us. I stare past her, keeping my face as blank as I can. Hiding my fear.

"Saunders! Step out here."

I'm standing as still as I can, but I realise that I'm clenching my fists because I'm worried about Saunders, and what Ketty is going to do. He walks out to where she's standing.

"Stand up straight, Saunders!" She barks. "Straighter! You're the line between life and messy death for those civilians out there. Try looking as if you could protect them from a bomber."

Saunders stands up straight, comes to attention, and looks dead ahead, past Ketty. She shakes her head. I'm holding my breath now, willing Saunders to get through this.

"It's like working with fluffy kittens. Grow some backbone, recruits!"

"Sir!" We all shout, as Saunders makes a final effort to stand tall.

She nods. "Better. Now, Saunders. At ease. I'm going to hand you the gun. Show me how you'll be holding it when you're on patrol."

Saunders stands at ease, and reaches out to take the gun. Ketty hands it to him, and he looks uncertain. My fingernails are digging into the palms of my hands, and I'm waiting for Ketty's reaction. He shifts the gun in his hands, then grips it firmly – one hand on the pistol grip, the other cradling the barrel.

"Not bad, recruit. Not bad."

I let out the breath I've been holding. Saunders is OK.

Ketty spends several minutes adjusting his grip on the rifle, then takes his shoulders and turns him round so we can all see what he's doing.

"This is a good grip. Watch and learn!"

Saunders isn't even trying to hide his relieved smile.

*****

We break into smaller groups, and one of the Senior Recruits brings each group a rifle. They're lighter than they look, with a tough plastic casing that makes them feel like something out of a sci-fi film. There are clips and toggles along both sides, and space for a large magazine of ammunition. At the moment, none of them is loaded – we're just getting used to handling them.

By lunchtime, the Senior Recruits have demonstrated how to take a rifle apart, clean and maintain it, and rebuild it. We've each had a turn, trying to copy their actions, and most of us have failed. The Senior Recruits have enjoyed shouting at us, and pointing out all the mistakes we've made. It's frustrating, and we're all ready for a break.

At lunch, I sit with Dan and Saunders. Their groups were like mine – entertainment for the instructors, while we get to feel inadequate and struggle with simple tasks.

"We'll get good at it. We'll be able to do it one day", says Dan, between mouthfuls of sandwich and gulps of water.

Saunders nods.

"We'll be training the next lot they bring in," I point out, "So we'd better learn fast."

*****

It was Dan who saved me on my first day at boarding school. We had both arrived early, before the first day of term. I was settling into an otherwise empty dormitory, and he had a boys' dormitory to himself for a few days as well. When I walked into the common room, the other girls sat together in giggling circles, leaning in, backs to the world, unwelcoming. Dan was the only person sitting alone, a dog-eared novel in his hand, feet propped on the chair in front of him. Even out of uniform, he was smartly dressed. Black trousers, a smart pinstriped shirt with the sleeves rolled up, untamed sandy-coloured hair framing his face.

I stood, uncertain, in the doorway. The girls in their groups didn't notice me, or if they did it was with a quick, dismissive glance. Dan, always interested in new people and new opportunities for discussion, looked up. He took his feet off the chair, and waved me over.

"Hey! Newbie!"

I gave him my best brave smile, and walked over to join him. It seemed like such a long walk to the far side of the common room, with everyone watching.

"Sit down," he said, indicating the chair opposite. I did. He held out his hand.

"Dan Pearce. Pleased to meet you."

"Bex Ellman. You too." I shook his hand, and sat back in the chair.

"So what brings you to our esteemed institution?" He waved his hand to indicate the wood-panelled room, the imposing fireplace, and the horrible orange-upholstered chairs that wouldn't look out of place in a doctor's waiting room.

So I told him my story, and he listened. That's what I needed, and that's what he gave me. At the end, he gave a whistle, and told me that I'd come to the right place.

"They're all about the education, here. You want to be a doctor? They'll love that. You're staying here all year? Even better. Bet you can pick up some extra tutoring in the holidays, too. Homework's a killer, but we have a system for that. You can join our study group, if Margie agrees. We're a man down since Ameen left last term."

I felt overwhelmed, but I nodded. It sounded good to have a support system – people who could help me, and people I could care for.

He leaned forward, his blue eyes sparking. "Do you want a sandwich? I want a sandwich. C'mon. I'll show you how to scavenge around here."

And he jumped up, took my hand, and practically skipped out of the room. The groups of girls glanced at us as we passed, and the giggling grew louder. I was only too pleased to be leaving.

Training

After lunch, the leaders march us to the other side of the camp, just inside the tall security fences. There's an assault course laid out, with walls to scale, water to run through, and barbed wire tunnels to crawl along.

Two of the Senior Recruits line up at the start, and a third, Jackson, explains the activity. He sets the recruits off, and narrates their progress through the course. By the time they reach the end, the recruits are soaking wet, muddy, and hardly breaking a sweat.

Then it's our turn. Group by group, Jackson sends us through the course, blowing a whistle to start us off, shouting instructions, and loudly shaming anyone who fails at any stage. After three attempts, we're allowed to walk round an obstacle and continue on the other side, but the leaders are keeping a close eye on all of us, and they know which of us needs extra training.

My turn. I walk up to the starting line with Saunders and two other recruits. We exchange nervous glances, and I look over at Dan, waiting to run in the next group. He gives me a well-concealed thumbs up and a grin. I grin back.

The whistle blows. My whole body aches, and I'd love to spend the afternoon sitting down and playing cards, but I need to forget the pain and concentrate on completing the course. I run to the cargo net and start to climb, fighting against its movements as the other recruits climb with me. At the top, there's a drop into a water-filled ditch, and I realise that I need to jump, right now. If I stop to think, I'll be stuck.

I jump, land in the ditch, and start to run. The water is freezing, and the shock takes my breath away. The blister on my foot is burning, but I focus, and push on. On the far side of the ditch, there's a wall. We'll need help to scale it, so I turn round and wave to Saunders. He's fighting the water with every step, but he acknowledges my signal and heads towards me. The other recruits are stopping, thinking about climbing the wall. I put my hands together into a stirrup, and offer Saunders a leg-up. He steps onto my hands, and I lift him until he can throw his arms over the top. He pulls himself up and over, and for a second I think he has jumped off the other side. I'm starting to shiver, and I don't want to admit defeat so early in the course.

There's a shout from above me, and I look up to see Saunders' head and shoulders over the top of the wall. He reaches down, and I jump up and grasp his hand. He drags me up until I can reach the top of the wall and pull myself over. There's a platform at the top, and all I want to do is lie here while I catch my breath, but I know I have to keep moving.

"You OK?" Saunders asks. I give him a nod, and a thumbs-up, and we both stand up. The recruit next to us is having trouble dragging his partner over the wall, so we reach over and drag her up. For the first time, I notice that Jackson is shouting as we head through each obstacle. He's shouting at us now.

"This isn't kindergarten! This isn't touchy-feely share time! Get yourselves through the course! Stop hanging around!"

I give the recruit we helped a quick encouraging squeeze on her shoulder, and reach up for the rope line above me. I swing my legs up, feet crossed over the rope, head towards the next obstacle, and start to drag myself hand-over-hand towards the other end. Behind me, the recruits in my group see what I am doing, and start doing the same, pulling themselves across the gap. There's more water below us, but I'm trying to concentrate on keeping the motion going, keeping my feet locked over the rope, and getting myself to the other side.

There's a wall ahead, and zip lines on the far side. I make it to the end of the rope line, and swing myself down onto the top of the wall, holding onto the rope for balance. I reach out for the zip line runner, and launch myself off the wall before I can think about it. The cold air rushes past and chills me through my wet clothes. The speed is exhilarating, but the cold is numbing my fingers. I focus on holding tight until my feet touch the ground, then I dig my toes in, ignore the pain from my foot, and start running.

I dive to my knees in front of the barbed wire tunnels, and crawl, as quickly as I can, under the rows of spikes. The ground is wet and muddy, and it's hard to move forward. I settle into a rhythm, keeping low, pulling myself forward with my frozen fingers. I can hear shouts behind me, but if I stop now I'll never find the rhythm again. I keep crawling.

I'm out. The barbed wire is behind me, and I'm nearly at the finish. Ahead, there are bars across the course – high bars to duck under, and low bars to jump over. I'm about to run ahead when I hear the shouting behind me.

I slow down and glance back.

Saunders and another recruit are standing on the top of the wall between the rope and the zip line. I can't see the fourth recruit, but she must be behind the wall, still attempting the rope crawl. Saunders and her partner are shouting, encouraging her to keep going. I turn around and take a step towards them, adding my own shouts to theirs. I hear a whistle, but I'm focused on walking round the tunnels to get close enough to help. The whistle sounds again, louder, and suddenly Jackson is in front of me, shouting in my face.

"Turn around, recruit! Turn around and get yourself to the end of the course! There's no time for teamwork here. You are responsible for your own safety. Turn around and clear the course. Now, recruit!"

I stop, and look past Jackson to where Saunders and the other recruits are finally together on the top of the wall.

"You can do it!" I shout, as loud as I can. "You can do it! Don't think about it – just jump!"

Jackson kicks out, and I feel my leg pushed out from under me. I land awkwardly, sitting in the mud.

"Get up, recruit!" he screams, his face red.

I get up, slowly. I can feel a bruise forming on my shin where his foot made contact. I avoid his gaze, turn myself round, and jog to the obstacle bars. Under one, over another. Under, over, under, over – I focus on the actions until I make it to the end, and run across the finish line.

I'm angry and I'm cold. I stand, shivering, while the others crawl through the tunnels and make it through the bars to the finish. I want to shout, I want to encourage them, but all I can think about is how cold I'm feeling, the blister on my foot, and the bruise on my leg.

And then Ketty is behind me. I expect her to shout, but instead she leans in and speaks quietly in my ear.

"Save your effort for where it matters, recruit. Leave the losers to lose."

I can feel her breath on my neck.

I shiver, and try not to react.

*****

Jackson sends those of us who are wet and cold off for a run to warm up while the last recruits complete the course. There's more whistle-blowing, and more shouting, but I'm concentrating on running without falling over. The recruits I've been helping catch up and run alongside me, talking in low voices.

"Thank you," says the female recruit. "You didn't have to help us back there."

I flash her a brief smile. "I don't think we're getting through this alone, whatever Jackson wants us to believe."

"Well. Thank you." We both run in silence for a while. "I'm Amy, by the way, and this is Jake."

"Bex."

We run round the training field, staying close to the fence and turning back past the dorms and the dining hall to the assault course. We make it back as the last group crosses the finish line.

*****

We're given twenty minutes to shower and change, and then we're back in the dining hall for a briefing. The rest of the afternoon is a theory session, explaining what they expect from us. Training in dealing with members of the public, training in defence scenarios, training in the message we are supposed to present.

The message is consistent. We are the front-line dolls. We are weapons in the public relations war. We are not here to fight the terrorists, we are here to make ordinary people feel safe.

If something happens, we are to make the protection of bystanders our priority. We must not think about rescuing each other. We are expected to make autonomous decisions, to look as if we are helping, and to keep ourselves visible. The government wants uniforms on the streets, and a ready supply of heroes if the TV cameras happen to catch a terrorist incident. Teamwork and helping each other are not encouraged. No one wants to see the front-line recruits on TV digging each other out of the rubble of a bombing. We need to focus on the civilians, and make their rescue and protection our automatic reaction.

They are making us expendable, and disposable. I wonder how many recruits and conscripts have been here before us – how many were sent out on patrols, and how many never came back.

*****

Dan's enthusiasm was infectious as he showed me round the school, pointing out classrooms and labs and music rooms.

"That's my favourite place to hide if I don't want to talk to anyone" he whispered, pointing up a steep flight of stairs to a deep window nook, overlooking the sports field. "There's a curtain you can pull across, and if you take a torch you can sit there after dark and read a book, or work on an essay, and no one would even suspect that you're there."

We reached the dining room, and he dragged me over to a table against the far wall. There was no one else around, but the table was set with bread, toasters, cutlery and plates, a kettle, and a pot of tea bags. Next to it was a fridge with sandwich fillings, fruit, drinks, yoghurt, and milk. He opened the fridge.

"What do you fancy? We've got cheese, ham, salad, some sort of spread ..." He held up a jar and squinted at the label, then put it on the table. "Peanut butter ... ooh! We should have peanut butter and banana sandwiches!" He picked up the peanut butter, and two bananas, and handed me a plate.

"The trick is," he proclaimed, busy pulling slices of bread from a bag, "not to skimp on the peanut butter. You need it nice and thick, so it's all sticky on your tongue".

He watched me scoop out the spread onto my bread.

"Come on! You need way more than that!" And he slapped another knife full onto my sandwich.

I started laughing. This was clearly the best sandwich I'd ever made, and I hadn't even tasted it yet. Dan quickly peeled a banana, and lifted a knife over it. He paused, and in a booming voice declared "I sacrifice thee to the deity of snacks!" He stopped, and looked at me. "Come on – you're killing the sacred moment!" He nudged my elbow until I peeled my banana, raised a knife, and declared the sacrificial ritual.

He gave me a happy grin, and sliced his banana into neat circles. He watched, approvingly, as I sliced mine, and then arranged the slices on the peanut butter.

We sat across from each other at one of the empty tables. He was right – it was a really good sandwich. We talked about him, and school, and what we wanted to do with our lives. He was in the same year as me, and we learnt that we both like history, and reading novels that grown-ups think are far too old for us. We were still sitting there long after we'd finished our sandwiches, and it was like discovering a crazy twin brother I never knew I had.

Company

After another hot meal, we're given an hour until Lights Out. I leave Dan playing cards with a group of recruits we know from school, and take a walk round the camp. The sun is setting, and the sky is blazing red and orange, with streaks of purple clouds. It's a beautiful evening, and so quiet after a day of being shouted at by the Senior Recruits.

I walk past the dorms and over to the gate, where two soldiers are guarding the entrance.

"Keep walking, recruit!" One of them shouts, and I wave, and move on. Close to the staff quarters and the kitchen, there's a picnic area with tables and benches. I head towards it, past the lights and music coming from the staff building, and sit on a table with my feet on a bench. I watch the sunset, trying to clear my head and make sense of what we're all doing here. We're not the army. We're not fighters. We're the front-line dolls. We're the cannon fodder and the government representatives on the street. We're worth nothing to the government, except as a way to make people feel safe. No one cares what happens to us.

It's up to us to care. It's up to us to look out for each other.

Someone coughs, and I notice a figure in the twilight, sitting like me on the next table.

"Hi," I say, raising a hand in greeting.

"Hi."

There's a pause, while we both watch the sunset, then the figure stands and heads towards me. It's a woman in her forties with close-cropped blond hair, wearing white kitchen scrubs and a purple fleece jacket.

"May I?" she indicates the table, next to me.

"Sure." I nod, and move over to make space for her. She climbs up and sits down.

"One of the recruits, then?"

I nod.

"So did you sign up, or did they kidnap you?"

I laugh. I haven't thought of it that way, but the realisation takes my breath away. I've been thinking of myself as a recruit, alongside the kids who volunteered.

"I guess I was kidnapped," I say, and my voice is a whisper.

She nods. "That's happening more and more. So where did they find you? School?"

My turn to nod, and look down at my hands while I process this idea – that I've been kidnapped and held against my will. I'm shaking, and I'm angry. There are tears in my eyes, and I can't hold them back.

My companion puts a hand on my shoulder, and lets me cry for a while. All the anger and frustration I've been carrying since they took us from school, all the tiredness and physical exhaustion – everything rolls over me in a wave, and I can't stop my reaction.

I've been kidnapped, and no one can rescue me. I'm disposable, and no one cares.

It takes a long time to calm down and catch my breath. I blink away tears, wiping my face with the sleeves of my sweater. Her hand is still on my shoulder.

"Thanks," I say. "Sorry."

"Don't worry about it. You're not the first, and you won't be the last. They have no right to grab you from school like that, and it's not right that you're here."

She reaches into a pocket, and brings out a can.

"Beer?"

I laugh, through the tears. She opens the can and hands it to me, pulling out another for herself.

"Is this allowed?" I ask, savouring the flavour of my first sip.

"Course not, for you. But I won't tell if you won't."

We sit and drink together as the sky fades to an inky blue.

"I'm Charlie, by the way." She holds out a hand for me to shake. I take it.

"Bex."

"Good to meet you, Bex."

"You too."

"You need anything, I'm out here most nights. I can't stand the noise." She jerks a thumb in the direction of the staff quarters.

"Thanks."

A whistle sounds from across the camp: ten minutes to Lights Out. I swig the rest of my beer, jump down and look around for a place to leave the can. Charlie holds her hand out.

"Leave it with me. And get back to your dorm – don't get locked out!"

I thank her again, turn, and run back across the camp.

*****

It was the start of term before I met Margie. She arrived early in the morning, just in time for the start of lessons. She took the last bed in my dormitory, as I was picking up my books and tablet for the day. Tall and slim, with long, dark hair, she radiated an air of relaxed confidence, as if this was her home, and we were the guests in it.

Dan met us at the bottom of the dormitory stairs, a stack of books in his arms, his uniform shirt sleeves rolled up to his elbows.

"Oh great – you've met. Margie, Bex; Bex, Margie. Margie's in our study group. Margie! Where have you been?"

Margie gave Dan a hug, slipping her books under one arm.

"Africa. The usual. I got back yesterday, but my Aunt's been holding me hostage. She wanted to make sure I got a shower and a decent meal before she brought me back to school." She looked over at me. "It's as if she thinks they don't feed us or give us proper beds to sleep in. She won't stop fussing."

We headed out into the corridor, Margie in the middle.

"So you've found us a new friend, have you, Dan? Don't tell me – he recruited you with one of his famous sandwiches."

I nodded, smiling, and she laughed and elbowed Dan in the ribs. "I knew it! So – what are you doing here?"

I explained, and she listened. Outside the door of the classroom, Dan stopped.

"Can she join the study group? Can she?"

Margie looked me up and down, and made an approving face. "I think so. Want to join us for study and occasional insanity?"

"I do, thank you!"

"You're in."

And I walked into my first lesson, already in the company of friends.

Armour

The next morning, we start again. Cross-country run, weapons training, lunch, assault course, theory, dinner, bed. The repetition is like hypnosis, keeping us distracted, making sure we don't think too much about what's happened to us and why we're here. By the end of the first week, we can all maintain a rifle, hit a target, complete the assault course, and perform basic public protection and interaction tasks. This is what they need us to do, and we're given no choice but to learn and train, and turn ourselves into their front-line dolls.

I try to take a walk every evening, just to clear space in the relentless schedule to do something for myself. Charlie and I make a habit of watching the sunset on clear days. I tell her about school – about Dan and Margie and Dr Richards. I tell her about Mum and Dad, and what it felt like to leave them behind. She listens, and tells me how brave she thinks we are, following orders and not making trouble. She always brings something for us to share – beer, chocolate, whatever she can smuggle out of the kitchen.

*****

Day eight, and the schedule changes. We've finished breakfast, and we're lining up at the gate for our run, waiting for the Senior Recruits to join us. Instead, Commander Bracken arrives.

"Recruits!"

"Sir!" We hurry to stand to attention.

"This morning's run is postponed. Follow me."

He leads us to the training field, where Robin and his clipboard are supervising the Senior Recruits as they lay out piles of grey plastic shapes. Batman blows his whistle and we line up, standing smartly to attention as he consults with his sidekick.

"At ease!"

We relax.

"This morning we are moving to a new stage in your training. HQ has sent us your armoured suits. Made to measure, and made to protect you when you're out on the streets. You'll be trying them on, and starting to train in them. Once again: your suit is yours. Look after it. Report and sort any damage. No changing it, no personalising it. Keep it clean, keep it functional. Keep it ready for use at any time."

Robin steps forward with his clipboard, calls us forward one by one, and sends us to a Senior Recruit. My turn, and he sends me to Ketty, who scowls at me and hands me a pile of lightweight plastic pieces, a set of tight-fitting black clothing, and a helmet with a tinted visor. I head back to my place in line, wrapping my arms around the armour and letting the helmet hang from my fingers.

I try not to think about what this means. How soon they'll be able to send us out on patrol. How quickly we're turning into their front-line dolls.

When we've all been kitted out, the Commander calls out a list of names – all female – and sends us to the dining room of the Senior Dorm. He sends the male recruits to the dining room in our dorm. We follow our Senior Recruits across the field.

Ketty is waiting when we reach the Senior Dorm. She watches us file in and line up, a sour look on her face.

"Recruits! Pick a table, put your armour down. Change from your fatigues into the fetching skin-tight thermal layer, put your boots back on, then wait for assistance. Now!"

We all rush to find a table, and begin to strip down. The base layers for the armour are lightweight and stretchy. I pull on the high-necked long-sleeved top, and sit down to take off my boots. There are gloves in the bundle, too, so I put those on, and the leggings. I put my boots back on and wait for a Senior Recruit to help me with the armour.

Ketty and three other women are working their way through the group, showing the recruits how to put together the armour from the pieces on the tables. They've started at the far end of the room, so I sit and wait for them to reach me. I watch the other recruits as they strap elements from the piles onto their legs, arms, and torsos.

The armour is sleek and shiny. There are panels for our shins and thighs, front and back; our forearms and upper arms, and front and back of the torso. There are additional, stretchy sections for our hips, knees, and shoulders; gloves with plastic sections over the backs of the hands; a utility belt with clips and loops; and a locking neck section that allows the helmet to click into place. There's a small canister that clips into the waist, and a series of clips and sliding fasteners in diagonal lines across the back. With the helmets on, the recruits already in their armour look anonymous and sinister. I guess that's the point.

I sort through the sections on my table while I wait. Leg pieces, arm pieces, torso, neck. The front torso section has my name printed on it in large letters, visible from a distance. The upper arms are printed with a Recruit Training Service logo. The left and right forearm sections have rectangular holes, surrounded by clips. I check the table, and the other recruits, but we don't have anything here to clip into them. The canister has a narrow, flexible pipe running from the top, which connects to the bottom of the torso section. The pipe runs up through the torso, and ends in a rubber seal, which matches a rubber seal in the neck section. Is this an air supply? What are they sending us to do that would need us to have an air supply?

Ketty reaches my table, and gestures for me to stand up. She sorts through the sections on the table, and begins to clip and strap my armour into place. She's rough, and she keeps snapping at me if I'm not standing still, or I don't hold pieces for her in just the right way. I do my best to do what she wants, but it feels as if I'm getting everything wrong. She pushes the last section into place, clips the canister to my waist, and connects the pipe to the torso. The assembled armour is comfortable, and lightweight, but it restricts my movements. It's going to take time to get used to wearing it.

Ketty hands me the helmet, and I put it on. She grabs it and twists it into place, pushing down hard against my shoulders. There's a click, and everything goes quiet. All the sounds in the room are muffled, and I'm locked away inside my armour. She gestures to me to remove it, and I struggle with the twisting action. She grabs it again, twists it, and pulls it off my head.

"Again, Recruit! Keep your finger on the catches on each side," she says, showing me the points on the edge of the helmet that activate the clips.

I take the helmet, push the clips, and twist it into place. A click, and the noise from the room becomes a background murmur. Ketty nods, pulls my visor up, and points to the recruits behind me.

"Line up," she says to me, and then louder: "Line up, recruits! We're heading back outside."

The male recruits are lining up on the training field as we jog out of the dorm. Standing to attention, the lines of figures in armour look impressive, and dangerous. These are the front-line dolls, the deterrents, and we look good. Armour in shades of grey and black, helmets with tinted visors. With the visors down, there would be no part of our skin on show – we could be robots, or proper soldiers. We've been designed for respect.

Commander Bracken strolls along the lines, inspecting us. He closes a clip here, adjusts a section of armour there, but mostly he nods at each recruit as he passes.

"Very good, recruits! You look the part. Now, let's see what you can do in the armour. Jackson!"

Jackson steps forward, still dressed in fatigues.

"Recruits!" he shouts. "Visors down, helmets off!"

We obey, clutching clumsily at our helmet catches, and stand, holding our helmets in front of us.

"Helmets on the floor." As I put my helmet down, I notice that my name is printed across the back. I'll be easy to identify wherever I am.

"Line up for the morning run. Today we're running in armour. Get used to it, and get going!"

We follow Ketty and the other Senior Recruits towards the gate, jogging awkwardly while we get used to the range of movement that our armour allows.

Today's run is shorter. We're still being shown off along the main road, but we don't run as far, and the cut back through the woods to the camp is not our usual route. I'm running the last section with Dan, talking when we can, and helping each other with the restrictions of the armour. We're coming up to the fence. We'd usually turn right, and run all the way round the training field to the gate, but today the leaders turn left, and we run past the staff dorm, and the picnic tables where I sit with Charlie. As we run, I notice a section where the trees continue past the fence into the camp, and the path we're running on pushes deeper into the woods. It's hard to see the fence from the path, but I'm sure I notice a gap between the fence and the ground. It's small, but the metal mesh curls up, away from the grass. I wonder whether a person could crawl underneath.

At the gate, we run past the guards and back to the training field. Commander Bracken is waiting, with three crates of guns. Our helmets have been removed from the field.

"Welcome back, recruits! Take a gun, and line up." We do as he says, and stand in lines, guns in patrol holds, as we've been taught. "Today's weapons session will teach you how your gun, and your armour, work together. Jackson!"

Jackson steps forward again, and Commander Bracken steps back to observe.

"Recruits! Space yourselves out, and pair up." We move apart, and I look round for Dan. Before I can find him, Saunders appears at my elbow.

"Hi, Bex! Want to pair up?"

I glance around, but Dan is out of sight. Everyone else is finding partners to work with. I shrug. "Sure."

We walk a short distance away from the nearest recruits, and wait for instructions from Jackson.

"How fantastic is this armour?" Saunders whispers. "It's so space-age! We look badass!"

I have to agree – even Saunders looks dangerous, and together we look as if we could contain a riot or lead a charge on a battlefield. I feel a surge of excitement, and I have to remind myself that that's not what we're here to do.

Jackson calls our attention back, and we turn to watch his demonstration.

The clips on the gun line up with the clips on the back of our armour. Left- or right-handed, it doesn't matter – there are clips on both sides of the gun, and in both directions across our armour. Jackson demonstrates on one of the recruits, and then tours the field, watching us practice in our pairs.

It takes a few attempts for me to get the hang of using the clips. There are magnets in the gun and the suit that help to set the position before the clips engage, but it is difficult to find the right angle as I reach over my shoulder and line up the gun. Saunders helps by guiding my gun for my first attempts, and after a while I can clip it in, almost every time. Unclipping it is easier, but still takes practice.

But Saunders is struggling. I try clipping the gun into place for him while he holds the stock, and letting him swing the gun round to find the magnets, but he really can't get it right. As his frustration mounts, his attempts become less and less accurate. He's starting to panic, and so am I.

"How do you do it, Bex? I just can't feel it. I can't feel how it's meant to be."

I make myself stay calm. I don't want him to know how badly he's doing.

"Try again. Just keep trying."

"But this is supposed to be easy!"

Jackson arrives, and I demonstrate my technique. Saunders looks terrified.

"Take a deep breath," I say, and I'm about to talk him through it again when Jackson mimes zipping his mouth and glares at me.

"That's enough, recruit. Saunders is going to show me what he can do. Saunders?"

And he tries. He really tries, but he can't get the action right. Jackson rolls his eyes, crosses his arms, and taps his fingers impatiently against his elbow.

Across the field, Commander Bracken blows a whistle, and calls us back. Saunders puts his gun into a patrol hold, and starts to run back, but Jackson puts out a hand and stops him.

"Again, Saunders."

I wait, willing him to get it right.

"Ellman, you're done. Get back in line."

I want to protest, but Jackson waves me away. I mouth a "sorry" to Saunders over Jackson's shoulder, and head back to the group. There's nothing else I can do.

We hand our guns to Commander Bracken, and he sends us back to the Senior Dorm to get changed. On the tables, with our fatigues, we find crates with our names on, our helmets already inside. We each have a cloth, a sponge, and a bowl of water. As I unclip my armour, I wipe each piece clean, polish it with the cloth, and place it into the crate. I fold up my thermal base layers, and put them into the crate as well, then get dressed in my fatigues.

Ketty stands at the door, watching us. When we're all dressed, she sends us back to our own dorm, with instructions to stow the crates under our beds, and report to the dining room for lunch.

As we queue for sandwiches and soup, I glance outside at the training field. Saunders is still there, with Jackson, trying and failing to clip his gun to his back.

*****

Saunders joins us as we line up for the assault course. He's missed lunch, but he looks happy. Jackson ruffles his hair as he sends him over, as if he's a puppy or a kitten, and I can't help feeling offended at the patronising gesture.

"Did you manage it?" I ask him under my breath, as we wait for a Senior Recruit to remind us of the personal best times we're aiming to beat.

He nods enthusiastically. "I did! And Jackson made me show him again and again, so I won't forget."

I'm about to congratulate him when he turns away, and I notice Amy stepping quietly through the group to stand beside him. He glances at her, and they share a

45

smile. Out of sight of the Senior Recruits, she slips her hand into his, behind his back. He interlaces his fingers with hers, and they both stand facing forward, hiding the gesture, but unable to hide the smiles on their lips.

I step back and fall into line. I'm surprised, and I'm trying to listen to the Senior Recruit, but my thoughts are straying. I'd assumed that Amy and Jake were together, but then I realise how often people have made the same mistake about me and Dan. I can't help smiling myself, seeing Saunders happy.

*****

Studying with Margie and Dan was an introduction to arguing about everything, but never falling out over anything. History was our favourite subject, and our favourite topic for debate, and we all brought something different to the discussions.

Margie was the activist. Her parents were somewhere in Africa, building schools and digging wells and trying to change the system that locked people into poverty. Your chocolate and bananas and tea had better be Fairtrade when Margie was around. She could always see another side to every debate, and she was quick to notice if a group of people had been excluded from the historical account. Her feminist critiques of Dr Richards' lessons were legendary. I always learnt something new when I studied with Margie.

Dan put his faith in the government. He was convinced that they had our best interests at the top of their priority list. He may have enjoyed finding places to hide from teachers and authority figures, but he trusted that the people running the country, and the world, were acting fairly and justly. He could always find an explanation for something the government had done, even when

Margie and I were shouting at him, and willing him to see the injustice.

I didn't know what to think. I didn't know that learning could be like this, and that people could get so involved and so invested in the world. I loved debating with Margie and Dan, and I loved that we could say whatever we wanted, and still be friends at the end of it. Homework had always been something I'd done in snatched minutes between looking after Mum, cooking dinner, and making sure I had a clean uniform to wear. That homework could be this important, and this interesting, was new to me, and I loved it.

Artist

We're back in the dining room for the briefing. Jake, Amy, Saunders, Dan, and me round a table in the corner of the room. There's a pile of questionnaires and answer sheets in the middle of the table, and a scattering of pens and pencils. We're waiting for the usual talk from one of the Senior Recruits, and maybe map and compass training, or some role-playing to get us used to dealing with the people we're supposed to protect.

Instead, Ketty walks into the room and switches on the TV. She uses the touchscreen to load a video for us to watch, and turns back to us to introduce this afternoon's activity. The room falls silent immediately.

"Today the government has decided to educate you all about the various weapons that you'll see in use when you're on patrol. Some, you might get to handle. Others, they want you to know that you must not touch. Those toys are not yours. Those are for the real soldiers. But don't worry, tiny fighters – you get some toys of your own."

I stare at the table, my anger rising. Ketty's doing it again – talking to us as if we don't matter. As if we're disposable.

"After the informative video, you'll have five minutes to complete the questionnaires in front of you. Don't screw this up. Identify the weapons, and identify whether they are for you to use, or for the grown-ups. This isn't rocket science, recruits, but it is important, so pay attention."

She sets the video running, turns out the lights, and sits down in a chair at the end of the table by the door. The recruits sitting with her sit up straight and angle themselves towards the screen, thinly disguised fear on their faces.

Dan and I exchange a glance across the table. This is new. We haven't been given detailed information like this before – we're usually learning how to calm a crowd, or help a frightened civilian, or contain a threatening interaction.

The video runs through the range of government-issued weapons and equipment. Our armour is shown, and our guns (safe for us to handle), along with black armour and riot shields (soldiers only). There's a rundown of the guns we don't get to use – everything from a small handgun to a machine gun mounted on the back of a truck. There are drones, and ground-based population-control devices, including the apocalyptically named 'City Killer' and the scurrying, spider-like 'Traffic Stopper'. There are see-through bullet-proof barriers (we get to put those in position and stand behind them), and crowd-control pepper sprays (we'll be issued those if we need them). The video runs through scenarios that we're expected to handle ourselves, and the tipping points where we're supposed to call in support from the army. Crowds turning violent, groups of terrorists staging multiple attacks, widespread collapse of infrastructure.

I glance round the table. This is more useful than I was expecting. There's more information about our job here than we've ever been given before. Next to me, Amy is staring, white-faced at the screen. Dan and Jake look worried, concentrating on the details of the images and the narration. And Saunders ... Saunders has a pencil in his hand, and on the back of one of the questionnaires, he's sketching. His attention is on his drawing, and on Amy.

She doesn't know she's being stared at. She hasn't noticed his gaze. She's giving all her attention to the TV screen. Saunders isn't listening to the video, and he's certainly not watching. My stomach sinks. He can't afford any more trouble today. Carefully, I reach out with my foot under the table and aim a gentle kick at his knee.

The table rocks, and Saunders looks up in surprise. I glare at him, and tip my head towards the screen. He looks at me, eyes wide, shaken out of his artistic concentration. I tip my head again, and he looks past me to the screen, realising what he's missing. Slowly, he puts the pencil down, picks up the sketch and slides it under the table, into a pocket, out of sight. He gives me a guilty look, and turns to watch the video, too late to pass the test. I turn back to the screen, wondering what I've missed.

Lucky for both of us, there's a very brief rundown to remind us about all the equipment at the end of the video. It might not be enough to give him a perfect score, but at least he's watching.

The video ends. Ketty stands up, and sends the recruit next to her to switch the lights back on. There's a murmur of discomfort as the bright strip lights replace the glow of the TV screen, and a scraping of chairs as people shift back to their tables.

"Grab a questionnaire. Grab an answer sheet. Grab a pen. Show me that you can watch a short video without falling asleep. No conferring. Five minutes. Go!"

We all reach for the question and answer sheets. Pens in hand, we work our way through the multiple-choice questions, confirming that we have understood what we have seen. I know all the answers, but I'm aware that five minutes isn't long to run through everything in the video. I check the clock on the wall. My heart is racing as I scan through the questions for anything I've missed.

Ketty is right. These are easy questions for anyone who's been paying attention. My hand aches from gripping the pen, but after four minutes, I've completed the task. I glance at Saunders, whose hand is hovering above the final few answers, his face a mask of panic. Dan drops his pen on the table and sits back in his chair. Jake picks up his sheet and reviews his answers.

Ketty is pacing the room behind me. I want to turn my head and check where she is, but I don't want to attract her attention. Carefully, I stretch out my foot under the table and nudge Dan's leg. He looks down, under the table, and then at me, puzzled. I meet his gaze, then look across at Saunders. Dan turns, and sees what I'm seeing.

Half a minute to go. Dan looks up, past my shoulder to see where Ketty is standing. He nudges Saunders, and starts to gesture under the table. Saunders stares at him, then looks down, and understands. He follows Dan's directions – thumbs up, thumbs down, counting on his fingers – until most of his answers are complete. Amy places her pen on the table as Ketty calls the end of the test. Saunders holds his in both hands, elbows on the table, trying to hide his shaking fingers. Dan gives him a final thumbs up, then gathers the answer sheets and lays them in a pile at the end of the table.

I realise that I've been holding my breath.

Jackson replaces Ketty at the front of the room, as Ketty collects the answer sheets and takes them away for checking.

"Recruits! We're going to revise our strategies for reassuring members of the public. Pair up!"

Our chairs shriek against the floor as we all stand up. Saunders points at Amy, who nods. I'm about to pair up with Dan, when I realise that Jake is looking lost, watching Amy as she walks round the table to stand with Saunders. I wave at Dan, and point at Jake as I move down the table. Dan nods, and looks for a partner at the neighbouring table, while I sit down next to Jake.

"Want to pair up?"

He looks at me in surprise, relief showing on his face.

"Sure. Thanks." He can't help glancing again at Amy and Saunders, who stand together, oblivious to everyone else in the room.

We spend the rest of the session role-playing our strategies for calming frightened people. We act as pairs of recruits on patrol, or as panicking members of the public. We keep switching who we're working with, staying in our pairs, but facing a different couple every time we move on round the room. Eventually, everyone has had the chance to demonstrate their calming techniques on Jackson, as well as on the other people in the briefing, and we're sent away for a bathroom break before dinner.

Dan finds me in the corridor.

"What was that? With Saunders?"

I tell him what I saw. Saunders, sketching Amy, while he should have been watching the video. Dan laughs.

"He's going to get himself into trouble."

I have to agree.

*****

We meet up again for dinner, Amy and Saunders sitting together, Dan with me, and Jake at the end of our table. We're halfway through tonight's stew-with-rice when Ketty walks in, tapes a sheet of paper to the wall next to the door, and leaves.

We exchange glances around the table.

"Results of the questionnaire?"

Dan and I stand up, and hurry to the door.

The list of names is arranged into passes and fails, and miraculously we've all passed. I double-check Saunders' name, but he's there with the rest of us. No penalties, no points lost for cheating. Dan and I exchange a grin.

Back at the table, we share the news, and Saunders slumps back in his chair with a sigh. He sits up, and offers Dan a high-five.

"Don't do that again!" Dan sounds serious as he slaps Saunders' palm. "No more lovey-dovey. Next time, watch the video!"

Saunders blushes and nods, and Amy gives him a confused look.

"He hasn't told you?" I ask, not bothering to hide my surprise. "Come on, Saunders. Show her what you were doing while the rest of us were studying government equipment."

Saunders squirms in his seat, obviously embarrassed, but he reaches into his cargo pocket, and brings out a folded piece of paper. Amy stares as he slowly unfolds it and hands it to her, her eyes growing wider as she takes it from him.

And it's good. Really good. Saunders can draw.

Amy holds the sketch in her hands as if it's the most fragile thing she has ever held. Saunders looks as if he's sitting on hot coals, waiting for her to comment. She looks at it for a few seconds more, then breaks into a beaming smile. She puts the sketch down on the table, throws her arms round Saunders, and gives him a gentle kiss on the cheek. He's grinning too, now.

Amy sits back in her chair and holds up the sketch to show us, hiding her face behind the paper. He's drawn her in profile, her face lit by the screen across the room, a strand of hair tucked behind her ear and another brushing against her cheek. It's a lovely, tender portrait of someone he clearly cares about.

"You're an artist!" It's all I can think of to say. "That's … beautiful."

He beams, proudly.

"Were you studying art?" Dan asks, "You know. Before."

Saunders nods.

"Art, photography, graphic design. It's what I want to do ... wanted to do."

"What can you do with that?" Typical Dan, whose options were always 'doctor, lawyer, Prime Minister'. I nudge him, hard, in the ribs.

Saunders shrugs. "I don't know. Advertising. Publishing. Illustration."

"That can still happen!" Amy sounds determined. "We're not going to be here for the rest of our lives. Things will get better! We'll go back to school." She looks around the table, meeting everyone's gaze. "Right?"

"You really want to go back there?" Jake asks, "With the decent meals and the stimulating education?" He smiles at his own joke, poking the remains of his dinner with his spoon.

"... and the not-going-running-in-armour, and the not-being-yelled-at-by-Jackson – and even Mrs Ashworth's English lessons!"

Jake groans, and rolls his eyes.

"You two were at school together?"

Amy smiles, shyly. "Next-door neighbours since we were a few days old. Same nursery, same kindergarten, same school all the way through. We were getting each other through boring lessons before any of you guys had met."

"Even Mrs Ashworth."

"Especially Mrs Ashworth!"

And they both laugh.

We sit at the same table all evening. It's pouring with rain outside, and even Charlie won't be out in this weather, so I stay and tell school stories, and learn about the people I'm training with, the people I'm helping. The people who are beside me when I need them.

Saunders picks up more paper and a pencil from somewhere, and starts sketching all of us as we're talking. There's a fantastic sketch of me and Dan, laughing, my hand on his shoulder as we tell everyone about trying to hide in the school library overnight. He sketches Jake, waving his hands to demonstrate the exact size of the snowball Amy threw through a classroom window while aiming at the back of Mrs Ashworth's head. From memory, he sketches us all in our armour, helmets at our feet, arms round each other's shoulders. He includes himself in that sketch, and hands it to Amy. She slips it under his first sketch with a smile.

She takes all the sketches, at the end of the evening.

JULY

Routine

So this is our lives. Morning run, in armour. Weapons training. Timed assault courses. Briefings and theory on dealing with the public. Rinse and repeat.

Every day, there are more reports of attacks and bombings, or attacks prevented by government forces. Images on TV of rebel fighters being arrested, dragged out of squalid hideouts, and thrown into the back of prison vans. I keep watching, hoping I won't see Margie's face among the fighters they're locking up.

The Senior Recruits show us the news broadcasts over dinner, every day. We need to know what the terrorists are capable of, what we are defending people against. We start to see recruits like us in the broadcasts, patrolling in their armour; walking in pairs and groups in high streets, sports grounds, and concert venues. At first, members of the public seem nervous around the recruits, but the armoured figures soon become a normal part of life.

The Prime Minister starts to broadcast daily messages. She's tough, and she refuses to negotiate with kidnappers and hijackers. The presenters are calling her 'our Iron Lady', and 'our generation's Margaret Thatcher'. They say this over and over, so it must be playing well with their audience.

There are show trials. Captured terrorists put on trial and the graphic details of their attacks shown on the evening news. They're always in handcuffs and prison jumpsuits, and they've always been beaten up. They have bruises on their faces, unwashed, unbrushed hair, and they look thin and ill. They don't get lawyers, and they don't get to speak except to plead guilty. They all plead guilty, and they're all sent to prisons or work camps, or Death Row.

It's terrifying, how quickly we all accept this new reality.

The message is clear. The Prime Minister reminds us that we're being protected. Something is being done. Democracy and freedom will be restored when the emergency is over.

I lose count of the number of times she reminds us of that, while the attacks only seem to get worse.

*****

Morning run. We're back on the long route again, now that we're getting used to wearing our armour. Across the bypass and the railway, and along the main road, where the people driving past can see us; through the industrial estate, and back through the woods. I'm running with Dan, talking when we get the chance. We're following a narrow path between the trees, dodging roots and muddy puddles.

Ketty pushes past.

"Up for a sprint, Dan?"

Dan glances at me, and I shrug.

"Sure", he says, and grimaces at me over his shoulder.

Dan and Ketty run ahead, and I take the opportunity to slow my pace and enjoy being outside in the woods. It's a bright morning, and I'm making good time. I take the chance to look around, and notice the trees, the deep green of the undergrowth, the birdsong. For the first time, I find myself thinking about how beautiful it is out here.

There's a shout from behind me, and I turn back to see what's wrong. I jog back along the path, towards a group of recruits, gathered round someone on the ground. My happy mood dissolves.

It's Saunders. He's caught his foot on a root and tripped. I reach the group, and see that his foot is twisted behind him at an awkward angle. I'm pretty sure it's broken.

Amy and Jake are standing over him. Amy is holding his hand, trying to help him stand. I grab his arm and haul him up, supporting his injured side. I look around for a Senior Recruit, but they're all ahead of us. We're the last runners at the back of the group.

"I've got you, Saunders. You OK?"

He grunts, and grips my elbow. I put his arm round my shoulders and wrap my arm across his back to support his weight. He holds the injured foot off the ground and hops along beside me as I start to walk.

"You guys should keep going. Run ahead and let someone know that Saunders is injured. Tell them we're coming."

Amy protests, but Jake takes her arm and gently pulls her away. They run on together, glancing back at us until they're out of sight between the trees.

It's just the two of us. I'm not sure we can make it to the gate, but I can't tell Saunders that.

"It's not far now", I say, wrapping my arm more tightly round him. "I've got you. Just keep moving."

His breathing is laboured, and he's obviously in pain, but we keep going.

It takes twenty minutes to get through the woods, but I can see the fence, and the route back to the gate. The bright sky has clouded over, and the day is looking grey and gloomy. We reach the fence, and turn along the short path past the camp. I can see everyone else lining up for weapons training, and I know we're going to be late, but we push on. Past the dorm buildings, past the row of army vehicles, and up to the guard post at the gate.

We're going to make it.

The gate is shut when we reach it. Two guards stand behind the wire mesh, staring out at the road behind us.

We walk up to the gate. The guards keep their eyes on the road, ignoring us.

"Let us in, will you?" I call out.

One of the guards looks at me, and shifts his gun to a combat pose.

"Seriously?" I shout. "We need to get to a doctor. Open the gate!"

"I don't know who you are. Orders are not to let any-one else in." And he looks away again, back at the road behind me.

This must be a misunderstanding. I help Saunders to sit down on the grass near the gate, then walk over and grab the metal mesh with both hands. I'm angry now, and I'm shouting.

"Hey! Open up!"

Both guards lift their guns and point them at me. I freeze, my hands gripping the gate.

"Back off! Hands in the air!" They both take a step towards me, keeping me in their sights.

I obey, lift my hands, and take a step back. I can't be-lieve they're doing this.

"We're late back from the run. You know who we are. Saunders needs a doctor – I think he's broken his ankle. Let us in, and we'll go straight to medical."

"Can't do that."

They're still pointing their guns at me.

They're serious. They're not going to open the gates. My hands are shaking, but I can't let them leave us out here. I can't let them leave Saunders here, in pain.

"Fetch someone to verify who we are! Just get us back inside."

The guards exchange a look, then one of them returns his gun to a patrol hold and walks to the gatehouse. He speaks to someone on a radio, and returns to the gate. The other guard keeps his gun aimed at me.

I'm looking down the barrel of a gun. I should be afraid, but my anger is stronger than my fear. I can't stop myself from fighting back.

"So?" I ask. "Is someone coming?"

The guard shrugs, and starts watching the road again, as if I'm not here.

I turn back to Saunders. He's sitting with his legs out in front of him, slumped over, head bowed. He needs a doctor, but there is nothing more I can do.

There are footsteps on the path. I turn back in time to see Ketty walking briskly towards the gate.

"Please ..." I begin, but Ketty's already talking to the guards.

"They're late. Leave them out there."

"How long?" asks one of the guards.

Ketty starts to walk away. "I'll let you know", she calls, over her shoulder.

Both guards resume their patrol positions, and focus their attention on the road.

I sit down next to Saunders, and put my hand on his arm.

"I'm sorry", I whisper. I can't think of anything else to say.

"I'm sorry", he says, through clenched teeth. He's fighting back tears, and I know he's in pain. I've got nothing to give him. I can't help. My anger and my bravery melt away as I watch the guards staring past us, guns ready.

I put my arm round his shoulders, and wait.

Kindness

It's lunchtime. We're still waiting for the guards to let us in. The grey sky has grown darker, and as we hear the other recruits heading back from the training field to the dining room, it begins to rain.

We don't take our helmets on the morning run, so we've got no shelter against the weather. Saunders sobs, and puts his head in his hands.

I can't watch him suffer. I stand up, and walk back to the gate.

"Hey!" I shout, waving at the guards. "Hey! Let us in!"

The guards ignore me.

I push my fingers through the mesh, grab hold of the wire, and start shaking the gate. The guards stare past me at the road.

"Heeeeyyyyyyyy!" I bellow, as loudly as I can. "Open the gate!" I shake the mesh as hard as I can.

The guards are still staring at the road, coat hoods up against the rain. I shake the gate again, and I catch one of them trying to hide a smirk.

The rain is matting my hair to my head, and starting to run down the neck of my suit. I can feel the cold water soaking into my base layers and tracking down my spine. My face is wet, and I'm having to blink the water from my eyes. We need to get out of the rain, and I need to get Saunders to a doctor.

I'm cold, and I'm furious. I keep shouting. I'm yelling, as loudly as I can, trying to attract attention. The guards look annoyed now – they're still pretending to ignore me, but I'm making their job impossible. I shake the gate again, and keep shouting.

*****

My voice is hoarse, and my base layers are soaked through. I'm shivering. I'm about to give up and sit down with Saunders again when I hear voices. I look up through the rain to see Commander Bracken running towards the gate with Ketty and the shift doctor. Ketty and the doctor are carrying a stretcher between them.

"Open up!" The Commander's voice cuts through the rain, and the guards run to open the gate. I step back, determined to get Saunders to safety. We're both shivering as I help him to his feet and guide him over to the stretcher.

"I think he's broken his ankle", I say to the doctor. He nods, holding one end of the stretcher while I help Saunders to lie down. Ketty holds the other end, and they set off together towards the medical centre. I try to follow, but Commander Bracken catches my elbow.

"Get yourself back to the dorm and warmed up," he snaps. "You're expected at the assault course in fifteen minutes." And he pushes me through the gate.

I stumble along the driveway, too cold and angry to argue or defend myself. I drag myself to the dorm, to my bunk, and force myself to peel off my armour, and the soaking base layers. I fumble in my locker for a towel, and try to rub some warmth back into my freezing skin. My hands are shaking, and it's hard to get dressed. I keep dropping my clothes, and tying my boots takes several attempts. I throw a sweater round my shoulders and sit on my bed for a moment.

There's a cough from the doorway. I've missed lunch, and everyone else will be heading out to the assault course now. I look up.

Charlie raises a finger to her lips, glances behind her down the corridor, and hands me a sandwich and a mug of hot chocolate.

"Get that inside you before you go back out in the rain," she says, quietly.

I'm so grateful, and I can feel the tears pricking at my eyes. I eat the sandwich as if it's the first food I have ever seen, and drain the hot chocolate as quickly as I can without burning my tongue. I'd like to sit here until I feel warm again, but Charlie gently takes the mug from my hand and pulls me to my feet.

"Go on. Get out there. You don't want any more trouble today."

I give her a quick, tight hug, drop my sweater on my bed, and force myself to jog down the corridor and outside, back into the rain.

*****

I make it through the assault course, and the afternoon briefing. At dinner, the Senior Recruits switch on the TV, and as we eat, we watch news of another bombing in Manchester. There are civilian casualties, and we watch recruits like us, in armour, dragging people from the wreckage of a shopping centre. I watch other recruits, doing what we're being trained to do, and for the first time I realise that I am afraid of what might happen.

It could have been us in the path of that bomb.

I look at the recruits around me, safe and warm after another day of training, and I wonder – what good are we actually doing here? Are we going to make a difference, as they tell us every day at the briefing, or are we just window dressing on something we – and the government – can't control?

Bruises

After dinner I head to the medical centre to see Saunders. Amy is there ahead of me. She barely touched her food, and left the dining room as soon as she could after the meal. Saunders is lucky – the doctor says this is a bad sprain, rather than a broken bone, and he'll be training with us again in a couple of weeks. For now he's stuck in the medical centre, and he'll be treated every day by a physiotherapist they're bringing in from the hospital in town. I wish him luck, and promise to visit him, before leaving the two of them together and heading out to see Charlie.

I'm just passing the corner of the medical centre. I can hear the noise from the staff dorm, and I'm smiling to myself because I know that Charlie will be outside, even though the rain hasn't eased completely. I want to thank her for bringing me lunch, and for getting me out to the assault course before anyone realised I was late.

I'm safe inside the camp. Saunders is with the doctor, and Amy is keeping him company. I've had a hot meal, and I'm wearing fresh clothes and a waterproof coat. I'm warm and dry, and I'm about to talk to Charlie.

There's a scuffing sound behind me, and before I can turn someone grabs my arms, and someone else clamps a hand across my mouth and another at the back of my head. White hot panic slams through me as I'm dragged off my feet and pulled backwards, kicking and trying to shout, but the sound dies in my throat. My heart is thumping in my chest, and I try to pull myself out of the tight grips on my arms and head, but I can't. I'm struggling as hard as I can, but the harder I fight against my attackers, the more they tighten their grip.

I can't believe how quickly I've lost control of my body.

They're dragging me backwards across the training field, and they're not stopping. I'm fighting panic. I need to escape, but struggling makes everything worse. I relax all my muscles, falling limp in their grasp and landing all my weight in their hands. It throws them for a second, and I nearly make it to my feet. I'm getting ready to sprint back across the field when they grab me again, and pull me onto the ground. I relax, and let them carry me, waiting for a moment when I can twist away and run again.

We're heading into the trees at the edge of the training field. The hands on my head loosen, and a voice next to my ear says "Don't make a sound", before lifting the grip on my mouth. I scream for help, but even as I cry out I know that we're too far from the dorms for anyone to hear me. Someone cuffs me hard across the cheek, and another voice whispers "Not her face!"

We're into the trees now, and I can't see the camp buildings any more. No one else knows I'm out here, and my heart races as the darkness closes in. There's a little light from the security lamps on the fence, but everything is reduced to shapes and shadows, grey on grey. We stop moving, and the person holding my arms pins me in place. They're strong, and I can't move except to kick, but my captors are behind me. I stay still.

There's a rustling sound, and an "All clear". The person holding me starts dragging me backwards again, then pushes me down to the floor. I'm lying on my back, pinned by my arms. I can't see my captors well enough to aim a kick or a headbutt, so I keep still, force myself to relax, and make it as hard as possible for them to drag me over the uneven ground.

The person holding me switches their grip to my shoulders, and gathers my coat and my T-shirt into their fists. They start to pull me backwards, and I realise that they're pulling me under the fence. The metal mesh scratches at my face and neck as they drag me through, my hands useless in the dark. I shout out again, and kick out hard, but there's nothing to connect with. I feel the edge of the mesh tugging across my chest and hips as they pull me underneath, the rainwater from the puddle under the fence soaking into the back of my T-shirt.

I'm through, and the second captor crawls through after me, grasps my arms again and pins me to the ground.

"You're in trouble, Ellman." And I recognise the voice. Ketty has dragged me out here to punish me – but for what?

"We keep telling you, Ellman. Save yourself. Don't be a martyr. Don't go helping the useless kids who can't make the grade." It's Jackson. "But what do you do? You make friends. You carry them home. You patch them up."

"You get us in to trouble."

"We don't like trouble, Ellman. We like things to run smoothly. We like recruits who do as they're told."

"You need to learn to do what we tell you."

And the first blow lands, hard, on my ribs.

So the camp isn't through with punishing me for helping Saunders. I'm pinned to the cold ground, and there's nothing I can do to stop this. I take slow, deep breaths, and try to disconnect from the beating that's coming my way. Ketty pulls my arms up, past my head, and pushes them into the mud with her knees. She leans her hands on my shoulders, and Jackson starts lashing out with his fists.

"Not her face!" Ketty says again. They're trying to hide this beating. The bruises will be under my clothes, so no one will know that this has happened. Jackson lands blow after blow on my ribs and belly.

It hurts. His fists are like explosions against my skin. I try not to give him the pleasure of hearing me scream, but I can't stop the grunts and gasps for air that mark my efforts to keep breathing. He's enjoying this, and Ketty is cheering him on. I try to take myself out of the moment – to think about other things. To hide from my fear.

Slam. I think about Saunders, lying in the medical centre.

Slam. I think about what would have happened if I hadn't helped him to get back.

Slam. Saunders, lying in the mud in the woods, waiting for help.

Slam. Amy and Jake, stuck on the obstacle course.

Slam. Dan, my only link to a life where I was happy.

Slam. Margie, who sided with the rebels.

The blows keep landing. The pain gets worse.

And then, suddenly, they stop. The grip on my shoulders disappears, the knees on my arms lift away. For a moment, I wonder what they're planning to do next. Fear keeps me frozen, lying motionless in the mud.

"You do this again, Ellman – you get us into trouble, and you won't be walking home."

They both stand up. There's a rustling as they crawl under the fence, and fading footsteps as they walk away, into the camp. I lie still, taking shallow breaths, waiting until I'm sure they've gone.

Slowly, carefully, I start to move. I pull my arms up, out of the mud, and down to my sides. I start to sit up, but it hurts too much, and I fall back, gasping. Gently, I touch my ribs with my fingertips, and the pain is everywhere. I feel sick. I think my entire torso is one continuous bruise. It doesn't run as far as my neck, or my arms, so no one will see what has happened with a casual glance, but the pain is real. This is exactly what they wanted – a personal reminder that I should obey orders, stick to my training, and ignore recruits in need. Right now, that's a tempting suggestion.

I roll onto my elbow, and sit up slowly. Every breath is a dagger to my injured ribs. I push myself up until I'm on my knees. I'm kneeling, and I'm fighting the compulsion to scream, in pain and frustration. Crawling, I drag myself back to the gap under the fence. I lie down, supported by my elbows, and drag myself through. The mesh fence claws at my back and legs, and my ribs are on fire as I pull myself underneath, grabbing handfuls of grass and heaving my body onto the camp side of the fence.

I'm through. I flip myself over and lie on my back, belly up. The rain has stopped, and the sky has cleared. I can see stars above the trees. I'd like to stay here, not moving, staring at the stars, but in the distance I hear the whistle that marks ten minutes until Lights Out, and I force myself to move. I pull myself to my feet, gasps of pain marking my progress, and set off across the field. I make it to the dorm with minutes to spare, strip off next to my locker and pull on the camp-issue pyjamas, trying not to cry out as I move my arms and ribs.

I'm tired enough that I fall asleep in spite of the bruising, and wake the next morning to stabbing pain – a reminder of what is expected from me at Camp Bishop. I've done my best. I've passed their tests and I've followed their orders. I've run and I've trained and I've worn their uniform.

But I've also helped my friends, and now I know what happens when I break their rules. It's all I can do not to burst into tears on my way to the showers.

Monitoring

For the next week, everything I do becomes a painful reminder of my lesson from Ketty and Jackson. Getting up, getting dressed, and moving around all hurt. Running is agonising, and the assault course is torture at every obstacle. I refuse to complain, or show them that I'm suffering, but my slower runs and assault course times show them that their punches hit their marks. Charlie smuggles me some painkillers, which help with the assault course, and with getting enough sleep, but the pain never really goes away.

I keep visiting Saunders after dinner every night. Amy's always there before me, and usually stays until Lights Out. Saunders has managed to find a supply of paper and pencils, so he spends his free time sketching, and gives his favourites to Amy.

After a week, he comes out to join the weapons training and the briefing sessions, and sits with us for meals. He's using a crutch for walking, and he's slow at moving around. While we're running or training on the assault course, he's in the medical centre with his nurse and his physiotherapist. I don't tell him what happened. He doesn't need to know.

Ten days after the attack, we're lining up for weapons training, dressed in our armour. Saunders joins us, still limping, and we're expecting another round of target practice and gun-handling drills. The Senior Recruits are standing at ease in front of us, two large crates on the ground in front of them.

Commander Bracken strides towards us, and everyone stands to attention.

"Recruits!"

"Sir!"

"Today we're filling in the final pieces to make your armour fully functional."

I glance down at the holes in both forearm sections.

"Today you will each receive a radio module, and a contamination panel. The Senior Recruits will help you to attach each piece to your armour, and then we'll begin training you to use them."

The sidekick hurries towards us, clipboard in hand, and calls out the list of names.

I step forward when my name is called. I'm given a black box from the first crate and a grey panel from the second crate, and I'm directed to where most of the Senior Recruits are standing. Jackson steps up to connect them to my suit. He flashes me an unfriendly smile, and gives me a playful sparring punch on the front panel of my armour. I try not to flinch away, but he laughs anyway. I swallow my anger, and keep my face blank.

"Left arm, Ellman." I hold out my left forearm. He takes the black box and pushes it into the hole in the armour. There's a click as it slides into place.

"Right arm." He clicks the grey panel into the hole on my right arm, then takes my hands, and holds them out in front of me.

"Left arm," he says, tugging on my hand. "This is your radio. Activate it by pressing the back of your glove." He takes my right hand and uses it to push one of the protective panels on the back of my left glove. A light comes on on the radio.

"Right arm is your contamination panel. Activate it by pressing the back of your right glove." He uses my left hand to activate the unit. A screen on the top of the panel lights up, showing three coloured bars. As I watch, the colours fade to white. "Red is chemical. Green is biological. Blue is radiation. White is good. Dark is bad. Keep it activated, and keep checking it. Understand?"

I nod, and try to take my hands back. He holds them out in front of me for a moment too long – a reminder of his power over me – then drops them and turns to the next recruit. I walk back to stand in line, my fists clenched.

We spend the next hour using the radios, and learning radio protocol. The microphone and speakers are built into the neck sections of our armour. They work best with the helmets on, but we can use them without. We split into groups and send messages to each other across the training field. We learn how to use different channels to decide who to speak and listen to. There's a scanning function, too. Hold the glove close to another recruit's armour, activate the scanner, and a robotic voice recites their name, rank, and unit.

Every fifteen minutes, the Commander broadcasts a radio message to everyone, instructing us to check our contamination panels.

"Contamination check: red!"

"Red: clear, Sir!", we all send back. The common channel is loud with our voices.

"Contamination check: green!"

"Green: clear, Sir!"

"Contamination check: blue!"

"Blue: clear, Sir!"

"Thank you, recruits. Continue radio training."

"Sir!"

It's distracting, but that's the idea. We need to be able to keep checking our own contamination levels when we're on patrol, and take action to protect civilians if we see any change on our panels. They're aiming to drill us in this, and make sure that we check our panels regularly, without being told.

And they do. Whenever we're wearing the armour – on the daily run, or during training – one of the Senior Recruits has the job of reminding us to check our contamination panels. Before long, I'm glancing at my right arm several times every day, even when I'm wearing fatigues. I catch other recruits doing the same. Commander Bracken called this the final piece that would make our armour ready for use, and I wonder when we will have the chance to use it on patrol.

I don't have to wait long to find out.

*****

"Recruits!"

"Sir!"

It's the evening briefing, three days after we plugged in our radios and contamination panels, and Commander Bracken is addressing us. I'm sitting with Dan and Saunders and Amy, and we're wondering what to expect.

"You have now had time to adjust to wearing your radios, and you've had time to train yourselves to keep checking your contamination panels. You're all competent with your weapons, and you can all run and train in the suits. It's time to send you out to do your jobs."

A murmur of excitement fills the room.

"There's an outdoor concert in Birmingham this Sunday. This will be your first assignment. The organisers are nervous about security. It's a big event, and they need you to be on patrol, looking out for anything suspicious, and safeguarding the people attending."

Anticipation and fear build in my chest as the commander talks. We're finally finding out what we're here to do.

"We've covered what this means. You've all trained hard to develop the skills you'll need to deal with the public at a large event. Be there, be visible, watch out for anything and anyone who shouldn't be there."

I think about the bombing in Manchester. Of the danger we'll be in. I think about our training, and the opportunity to use what we've learnt.

The opportunity to be the government's front-line dolls.

"We'll run through all your training again over the next few days. On Sunday, you'll assemble here at oh-six-hundred for breakfast. Wear fatigues, and bring your armour and helmets. We'll assign each of you a weapon before we leave – this will be your personal weapon from now on. Protect it, maintain it, keep it safe at all times. Report any issues to me.

"Questions."

Everyone's hands shoot up.

*****

"It began with bombings. People with grievances against our policies, or our way of life, the way we were interpreting religious books. Every couple of weeks there'd be a bombing, somewhere in the country. A few civilians would be killed, some people injured, and everyone would be outraged. The government would say that they were tracking the terrorists, that they had credible intelligence, or that they'd made some arrests, but nothing stopped the attacks."

Dr Richards' History lessons were strictly controlled. She could talk about things that happened a long time ago, but she couldn't talk about the background to the terrorism we were watching on the news every day. Dan and I knew that Margie was talking to her privately, usually at weekends when most of the teachers were away from school.

One evening, Margie talked her into joining us in the library. We waited until everyone else had left, and then Margie asked her to explain our most recent history. Why the government wanted people like us to volunteer, to join the army and fight the terrorists. Dr Richards was young, and passionate about her subject. She made me feel excited and involved in whatever she was talking about. She was always smartly dressed in a short skirt and blouse, with her long brown hair tied neatly back. And she was genuinely interested in what we had to say.

She leaned forward in her chair, elbows on the table, and started at the beginning – long enough ago that we couldn't remember the details.

"There were more bombings. There were a couple of nasty hostage situations and some personal attacks against people in power. Slowly, the government started to take away our powers. Scotland saw what was coming, and voted for independence, but that left the rest of us to deal with the attacks and the government crackdowns."

"Why did anyone put up with that? Taking away democratic rights?" Dan sounded grumpy and impatient. Dr Richards shook her head.

"People were happy to see them go. People were happy to co-operate with anything that kept the danger away, that kept their children safe – that meant that their lives could continue."

I tried to imagine trading rights for safety. We all had a vote on the school council, and I couldn't imagine giving that away so the school could make decisions for me. "Why? Why would anyone let that happen?"

"Think about it. Think about your lives. The lives of people out there. Safety at school and at work. Sports, shopping, coming home safely at the end of the day. They – we – accepted all that in exchange for our rights to demonstrate, to protest, and even to vote."

"But we'll get our vote back, when the bombings stop." Dan was sure of himself. This was his favourite subject.

"Maybe. I hope so." Dr Richards sounded uncertain.

Patrol

It's Saturday night. We've had our final training before the concert tomorrow. The sense of excitement increases during dinner, everyone talking and laughing, anticipating the change of scenery and routine. I eat, and listen to the people I've been training with bragging about how good they'll be at real work, how they'll be great at keeping people safe. I wonder whether they've really understood what our role will be. Front-line dolls in fancy costumes, making people think they're safe. Visible distractions from the real work – from the police and the army behind the scenes. Targets for terrorists. Disposable.

I slip out of the room, and take a walk to the picnic area. Charlie is waiting, beer in hand, sitting on one of the tables. The sunset is disappointing this evening – shades of blue and grey – but we watch it anyway. She hands me a beer as I sit down beside her.

"I hear you're getting out of here tomorrow."

I nod.

"Just for the day. We'll be back in time for Lights Out. We've got the daytime shift."

"First time on active duty?"

I nod.

"Are you ready?"

I think about it – about what we'll be expected to do.

"We're not actually fighting terrorists – we're there to make people feel safe." I shrug. "So I guess we're ready. We just need to look convincing."

Charlie laughs.

"I reckon you're just what they need. That armour of yours makes you all look like space-age ninjas. I think I'd be happier walking down the street if I had a space-age ninja looking out for me."

I can't stop the grin that is spreading across my face.

"Yeah. Badass ninjas. We're gonna rock."

*****

Up. Shower. Dress. Stuff my cargo pockets with any-thing that might be useful. I pull the armour crate out from under the bed and haul it down the corridor to the dining room, where most of the recruits are already standing round, waiting for their day off site.

I drop my crate next to my usual table and join the queue for breakfast.

Saunders lines up behind me. I'm surprised to see him here. He's still limping, and he's not doing any physical training with the rest of us yet.

"You're coming with us?" I ask, while someone fills my tray with food.

He grins.

"The Commander signed me up himself! He says he's got something in mind for me to do. So yeah – I'm coming with you!"

His excitement is evident. We all assumed that he'd be spending the day here alone. He's thrilled to be part of our first assignment. To be a target, with the rest of us.

I force myself to smile back.

*****

There are two coaches waiting at the gate when we line up with our crates and file out of the dining room. The Senior Recruits have handed us each a gun to pack with our armour, so we're ready to start our first day on active patrol.

We line up to stow our crates in the luggage section under the coach. Batman and Robin are overseeing the operation, and the sidekick ticks us off the list on his clipboard as we climb on board.

I find a seat next to Dan, and we talk about school trips we've been on together: field trips in coaches like these, off to learn about the history of the industrial revolution, or the geography of coastal erosion. This feels different. There's excitement in the air, but with it comes a sense of unease. We don't know what to expect from our first day on patrol, but we all know the dangers that we're there to protect against. In an hour or so, we'll be on the front line, showing the public that there's nothing to worry about. That we're protecting them.

The reality of our assignment is sinking in, and the closer we get to Birmingham, the quieter our conversations become. The novelty of leaving the camp is wearing off, and our attention is shifting to the dangers of the day ahead. I keep thinking about the Manchester bombing. About the recruits, pulling people from the wreckage.

There's silence on the coach as we pull into the backstage car park. Dan takes my hand, and I grip his fingers tightly. We look at each other.

"We're going to be OK."

I nod. "We're going to be OK."

*****

The next hour is crazy. We all help to shift the crates from the luggage space under the coach to our base of operations – a marquee at the end of the car park. I find my own crate, and follow the other female recruits to our changing area. Out of fatigues, and into base layers and armour. We pack our clothes into our crates and stack them out of the way, then line up in the marquee for the briefing.

Batman and Robin are here, supervising our activities. The Commander's briefing is short: follow orders from anyone in uniform. Be visible, be approachable, be well-behaved. Use our guns only if strictly necessary, and only in self-defence, or in defence of civilians. Report anything suspicious, but don't investigate – that's the army's job. In case of emergency, save ourselves, save civilians, rendezvous in the car park.

The sidekick consults his clipboard, and pairs us up for patrol duty. I'm with Amy, and we're assigned to patrol inside the event, walking round the edge of the concert crowd and helping people to feel protected. Front-line dolls.

On our way out of the tent, we're sent to radio control for an equipment check. Jackson is running comms, sitting at a folding table with the field radio and headset, Saunders in fatigues next to him with a clipboard and pen. Jackson grabs my left hand, activates my radio, then motions for me to put the helmet on. He tests my receiving and broadcast status with minimal conversation, then moves on to Amy. I take off my helmet, and turn to Saunders.

"So this is what the Commander signed you up for!" Saunders grins.

"Isn't it great? I'm right in the middle of everything that's going on, but it's an indoor job with no walking. Plus you guys can tell me what it's like out there, so I won't miss anything." He seems genuinely happy.

I smile, tip my head a fraction towards Jackson, and whisper "Good luck!"

Jackson gives Amy a thumbs-up signal, then assigns us our own private channel so we can walk and talk with our helmets on. Amy flashes a quick thumbs-up to Saunders, who smiles and waves.

"Brown! Ellman!" Commander Bracken waves us over to the door of the marquee. He straps a broad fabric band round the armour on my upper arm, slips a security pass into the windowed pocket, and does the same for Amy. "You're up. Through the security gate and round to your left. You'll come in at the back of the arena. I want you patrolling the perimeter every half hour. Keep up a steady pace, walk all the way round; keep going until we call you back."

"Yes, sir!"

"Helmets on. Guns in your hands." We obey, and he inspects us before waving us out of the door.

This is it. This is what we've trained for. I will myself to stay calm as we march out into the car park.

*****

Dr Richards continued her explanation, speaking softly in the quiet library.

"The government recruited and trained new soldiers, and gave them the job of policing the country. Unlike the police, the soldiers carried guns. We were told that the good guys had nothing to worry about, and that the soldiers would allow us to carry on with our lives without fear."

"Well – the good guys don't have anything to worry about. Why would the soldiers pick on someone minding their own business?"

Margie rolled her eyes at Dan. "Why wouldn't the 'good guys' want to protest about something they can see is unfair? Why can't the 'good guys' make a stand against things they think are wrong? And how do the soldiers know who the good guys are? You could be standing next to a bomber, and it could be you who gets shot! But you think you're a 'good guy', right?"

Dan rolled his eyes in response, and Dr Richards put her finger to her lips.

"Keep your voices down!"

"So how did we get here?" I whispered, glancing round at the empty library. "How did we get to the government asking us – asking sixteen-year-olds – to sign up and join their army?"

"Well, first the language started to shift. We'd all been sure that the attacks were coming from foreign groups – extremists, people with grudges against the UK. The government cracked down on immigration, and restricted foreign trade and foreign travel. But the news began to talk about attacks by British rebels. People who wanted an end to austerity, an end to fat cats and bankers' bonuses."

"So we're fighting ourselves?"

"This whole country is a battle ground," said Margie, her voice grim. "It's civil war. Anti-austerity, pro-Europe, anti-government."

Dr Richards gave Margie a stern look. "You know we can't use that term. Whatever this is, the government will never allow it to be called a civil war."

Margie sighed.

Public

The arena is empty when we're waved through by civilian security. It's a wide expanse of grass surrounded by tall metal fences on two sides. There are buildings on the side next to the car park, and at the far end, a stage with racks of speakers and giant screens. There's a large sound control booth close to the buildings. The audience hasn't arrived yet, but we're officially on patrol. We start our slow, measured walk around the perimeter of the field.

"What are we doing here, Bex?" Amy sounds baffled. "What are we supposed to be doing?"

I look around at the empty field. I can see some activity on the stage – teams of people are setting up equipment – but there's no one else here. Everything seems safe. Everything feels normal.

"I guess this is an easy first assignment. They're breaking us in gently."

Then I notice the camera crews. There are people with cameras on the stage, and another camera crew on the roof of the building next to the field. I look up at the sound booth as we pass, and there are two more cameras here, tracking our progress round the arena. The camera crews should be testing their views of the stage, but as I look around I notice that they are all trained on us, tracking us as we patrol. It's uncomfortable, knowing that we're being watched.

"We're on display, Amy. They're filming us for news broadcasts. They want people to see that we're here, protecting them. That it's safe to come out and enjoy themselves."

Amy straightens slightly, and walks a little taller.

"Let's put on a good show, then!" She says.

*****

We've been patrolling for about an hour when the first people start to arrive. There's a queue forming along the outside of the long fence, and the concert-goers are watching us through the metal mesh. We're not the only people on patrol – three more pairs of recruits are slowly making the circuit of the field, spaced apart so that we are always covering a different section of the arena. The people in the queue are taking photos and videos of us as we walk. More recruits patrol up and down the queue on the outside of the fence, and there are more outside the park, making sure they are visible on the approach to the concert.

Screaming guitar chords from the sound check are loud enough to make me jump, and Amy raises her gun before we both realise that we're safe. The people in the queue cheer loudly, and the sound check continues. Most of the cameras turn to the stage, but a couple are still trained on us, following our steps around the arena. I can't forget that we're on display.

When the gates open, the crowd comes running in, and Amy and I are forced to stop and wait for the stream of people to clear before we can continue our patrol. Someone in the queue notices us standing there, and stops, throwing his arms out to hold back the people around him, and nodding to us to continue. Holding my gun in one hand, I wave a thank-you to him with the other, and we walk through the space, feeling like superheroes in a movie.

"That was awesome!" squeaks Amy. "It's like being famous!"

"I think it helps that we're the ones with guns."

"True. But they really seem to like us."

"They've been told that we're here to protect them. Of course they like us. They think we're going to save their skins. And we are wearing the coolest armour."

"We really are." I can hear the smile in her voice, and I notice the swagger in her steps.

The crowd flows through the gates, pushing up to the front of the arena, jostling for the best view. At the front, we patrol on the empty side of the barrier that keeps the crowd at a safe distance from the stage. As we walk in front of the crowd for the first time, we notice the noise, but also the looks we are getting from the people in the front row. There's a woman with her hands pressed together in a gesture of thanks. A man who takes his baseball cap off and holds it to his chest as we pass. People who shout or mouth 'thank you' at us as we walk.

They think we signed up for this. They think we're volunteers. They are confident in our ability to protect them.

I think about Manchester, and I don't know whether to laugh or cry.

As we continue to circle the field, people step out from the crowd to thank us, to shake our hands. Someone tries to give me a hug, over my gun. People reach out to touch us on the shoulder and the arm as we walk. I shouldn't feel threatened – I'm the one with the gun and the helmet – but I'm feeling overwhelmed by the attention, and the incredible number of people in the crowd. I realise that I have probably never seen so many people in one place. On television, maybe, but never in a place where I'm standing. I can feel my breathing getting faster, until I'm fighting panic. More and more people reach out to thank us, and I have to focus on what I'm here to do. I look straight ahead, clasp my gun tightly, and keep walking.

Amy's voice in my ear is a constant stream of whispered 'thank you's as people approach us. Her voice sounds choked, and I realise that she's in tears.

"Amy? You OK?"

"I never knew, Bex. I never knew. What do they think we can do for them?"

"We're here for show, Amy. Walk tall. Keep walking. Give them what they want."

They want protectors, and they want to say thank you. They've been told about the brave young people who signed up to defend them, and they want to thank us for putting ourselves in harm's way. For allowing them to continue living their lives. They've probably seen films of recruits in training, and major cities are constantly patrolled by people in armour like ours. They've also seen the same atrocities we have on the evening news.

I tell myself to keep walking – tell Amy, too. We keep going, the centre of a moving crowd of grateful civilians.

When the music begins, it's a relief. The crowd turns its attention to the stage, and we're left in peace to walk and patrol the edges of the space.

"They're just having fun." Amy says eventually, wonder in her voice. "They don't have to worry about anything. They get to come out and listen to music and dance and scream. They're not thinking about the next attack."

I look around at the crowd.

"They can only do this because we're here. We are the ones who make this possible. It sucks for us …"

"It really does!"

"… but this is what we do, Amy. This is what we've been training for. And one day, we'll be able to go back to this ourselves."

I almost believe it.

*****

It was dark outside the library windows as Dr Richards continued her private lesson. We huddled round the table, listening carefully to her insights, her voice barely above a whisper.

"The rebels changed their tactics. The attacks on politicians became personal, with terrorist groups targeting well-paid ministers and demanding that they stopped taking rights and benefits from the poorest in society. There were some kidnappings. Some nasty stuff happened, and the government needed an excuse to crack down on everyone. Good guys and bad guys – they just wanted to take control.

"The Crossrail bombing was the trigger. After the bombing, the government declared a state of emergency. They put themselves in power indefinitely, with the permission of the King. No more elections, no more votes. They brought back the death penalty for terror attacks. They took away civilian mobile phones, private Internet access, social media. I know that doesn't mean anything to you, but to anyone a little older than you are, that was like losing the air we breathed! They claimed that their role was to protect us until the emergency was over, but their aim was to shut down any communication that they couldn't monitor. They tapped all the landline phones, they started reading private mail.

"They took away our freedom, but they did it gradually, and they sold it as a good thing at every stage. No one doubted that the new terrorists were home-grown, and that it was the job of the government to stop them."

"So why don't we know about any of this?" I was trying to figure out what I knew already, and how Dr Richards' explanation fitted with my experience. I was too young to remember most of this, and I realised that before I met Margie and Dr Richards, I hadn't been paying attention.

"They don't want you to know. Do you know what would happen to me if anyone overheard this conversation? The government took precautions to make sure you only ever hear their side of the story.

"Quietly, at the height of the panic, the government took over the news. So now the Public Information Network is the only news service allowed to broadcast. We used to have dozens of news channels, and radio stations, and they all had their own views on what the government was doing. But the government couldn't control their message if there were people out there challenging it. They sent censors to all the newspapers to make sure their news was pro-government. There are still rumours of journalists disappearing, and reporters being arrested while researching stories."

Margie cut in, sounding angry. "They told us that all this was to protect us. And most people were grateful, handed over their rights, hugged their children, and carried on."

Dr Richards nodded.

"Exactly. Take freedoms away slowly enough, and demonstrate the benefits of censorship, or a strong government, and people will queue up to give those rights away. If the reward is reassurance, or an easy life, or safety for their children, and the rights are taken away piece by piece, people let it happen."

"But what about all the TV channels that aren't showing news? All the books and theatres and shows? How are they still allowed to run?" Dan was trying to find a hole in Dr Richards' argument. Something he could use to demonstrate that her theory was wrong, and that the government was acting in our best interests.

"They're heavily censored. There are TV shows and films we used to take for granted, that no one is allowed to show now. Instead, you get plenty of big-budget entertainment. Plenty of escapism. Plenty of carefully edited

'Reality TV'. Big concerts from approved bands with carefully curated playlists. Feel-good song-and-dance shows at the theatre. Plenty of pubs and clubs and decent beer. The government made sure the people were entertained, and most of them didn't even notice the changes, until one day they woke up and they couldn't vote."

Anger

We're rotated out of our patrol route for a lunch break, then we take someone else's place patrolling the public car park. It's quiet out here with our helmets on. We can hear the music, but the noise of the crowd is faint and distant.

We walk up and down the rows of cars, keeping a look out for anyone who shouldn't be here. There are security guards at the entrance, so this should be a zone for ticket-holders only, but we patrol anyway.

"I meant to say, Bex … thank you … for what you did when Saunders fell."

She's looking straight ahead, as if she's concentrating on the cars in front of us, but I realise she's been trying to say this for days. I try to hide my surprise.

"I did what I could. I wasn't going to leave him in the woods."

"But Ketty, and the guards …"

I interrupt. This isn't a conversation I want to have. What happened, happened. I can't change anything by running through it again, and I don't want to provoke the anger I'm still feeling. Not here.

"It's fine, Amy. It's what happens if you break the rules. They don't want us looking out for each other – they want us looking out for the public. The people in the arena. But we can't do this alone, and I'm not going to let them tell me how to treat my friends."

She turns, quickly, to look at me, and turns back to focus on the ground ahead. I think the conversation is over, but then she whispers, barely loud enough for the radio to pick up.

"I know what Ketty and Jackson did to you. I know Ketty hates you for helping the rest of us – you've got her into trouble because her recruits aren't sticking to the rules. Thank you, Bex. Thank you for sticking up for us, even when they …"

She sobs, once. I reach over and take her hand, and she gives my fingers a squeeze.

*****

Our first circuit of the car park takes us back to the arena entrance, and a group of event staff taking a break. We nod to them as we walk past, and a man steps forward, blocking our path. Amy brings up her gun, and I switch my radio to the general channel, trying to sound calm and brave.

"HQ, please advise. This is Ellman and Brown in the car park. Member of staff is blocking our path."

The man looks at Amy, then raises his hands in the air to indicate that he isn't threatening us. He turns to show us a professional-looking camera clipped to his belt, and points to it, and to us. I notice a 'Press' security pass hanging on a chain round his neck.

"HQ, update. It's a press photographer. He wants photos of us. Please advise."

"Ellman. Go ahead. Let's make some beautiful publicity photos!" It's Jackson, and I'm sure I can hear laughter in the background before he cuts his microphone. I can't help rolling my eyes.

I switch the radio back to the private channel, and tell Amy to stand down. She lowers her gun. The man looks relieved, and mimes removing a helmet. I clip my gun to my back, twist my helmet off, and tuck it under my arm. Amy watches, and then does the same, turning away briefly as she wipes her eyes with the back of her hand.

"Ladies!" says the photographer. "Mind if I catch a few shots of our brave RTS volunteers?"

"HQ says that's fine," I answer, partly to him and partly to reassure Amy.

He waves us over to stand in front of the security fence, then asks us to hold our guns in one hand and our helmets in the other. He takes a few photos, then takes our helmets from us and puts them down on the grass next to his feet. He asks us to hold our guns as if we are on patrol. More photos.

Standing in the open without my helmet is making me nervous. I need to calm down and focus. This is what we're here for – we're on show. We're here to convince the public that they're safe. I'm armed, but without my helmet I'm an individual. I'm a target.

I need to become anonymous again. I need to look like a trained soldier, not a pretty face in a uniform. He keeps taking photos, and I can feel my anger growing.

I'm not a model. I've endured running and training and punishment – for what? This man doesn't care that I can fire a gun and get through an assault course. He only cares if I look good in my armour. I want to walk away, but my orders are to pose for photos.

I can't let him see how angry I am. I stand up straight, stare past him, and wait.

He takes his last photo, then crouches down and picks up our helmets. He steps forward and hands them back to us, a cheerful smile on his face. I force myself to focus on what he's saying.

"Thank you, ladies! Great photos. Thank you for your service!"

Amy thanks him, but I can only nod as I lift my helmet back over my head and lock it in place. I reactivate the radio, and try to keep the anger out of my voice.

"Come on, Amy. We need to keep moving."

*****

We patrol the car park for an hour or two before we're rotated out again for a break. Helmets off, we walk back to the staging area. Jackson greets us at the door of the marquee, loud enough for everyone inside to hear.

"Is it? Can it be? Let me fetch my camera – it's Soldier Barbie and her bestie!"

There's a wave of laughter from inside the marquee, and Jackson watches us as we walk past.

"Work it, Barbie! Work it!"

Amy laughs, but I focus on getting away from Jackson. I know we're only here to give TV shows and newspapers something positive to report, but I'm really angry now. We've done as we were told. We've patrolled and accepted thanks from the crowds. We've posed for photos, and we've behaved perfectly for the TV cameras. I know we're fake soldiers. I know we're not here to fight, but suddenly this all seems so pointless. I was kidnapped from school for this, and so far I've done what they've asked me to do. I'm being laughed at for playing along, and I've been beaten up for showing compassion to the recruits around me.

We're all just trying to get through this. We're all waiting for the situation to improve, for the terrorists to stop their attacks. Waiting to go home, to go back to school, to have our normal, teenage lives back. And Jackson is mocking us.

I want to fight. I want to break something. I want to shout and scream and tell the cameras outside that this is insane. That I want my life back.

I take myself to the far corner of the tent and pull a bench up to one of the folding tables. I put my helmet down next to me, and unclip the gun from my back. I take several deep breaths, then start taking the gun apart. This is a task I can focus on. I need to move slowly and carefully, and I need to ignore everyone else in the marquee.

Safety on. Unclip the magazine, lay it neatly on the table. Unclip the pistol grip. Slide the handguard off the barrel, unscrew the barrel from the gun. Slide the stock up and away from the central section. Slide and unclip the elements of the central section, lay them out neatly on the table.

This is calming. This is helping. I lay my hands, palms down, flat against the table; close my eyes, and take some more slow, deep breaths. Then I pick up the last pieces I dismantled, and start to attach them together again, checking each piece for dirt and damage as I go. Slowly, carefully, I rebuild my gun, pick it up, and sight down the barrel at the wall next to me. And then I take it apart again.

I don't know how long I spend, disassembling and rebuilding my gun, but when I clip it onto my back and turn around, Amy has gone. The tables and benches are mostly empty, but Jackson and Saunders are still at the radio table. Jackson is talking and listening on his headset, but Saunders is watching me, his face serious. He gives me a thumbs-up/thumbs-down signal, and waits for me to answer. I wobble my hand, and I'm about to head over to talk to him when Commander Bracken stands up from a table across the marquee and walks over to where I'm sitting. I realise he's been watching me.

"Ellman!"

"Sir!" I shout, standing up.

"Back with us now, are you?"

"Yes, Sir!"

"Something bothering you?"

I risk a quick glance at Jackson, who is looking very busy with the radio.

"No, Sir."

"Doesn't look that way to me, recruit."

"No, sir."

"Have you finished taking it out on your gun?"

"Yes, sir."

"Good. Go and get changed, Ellman. You're done with patrols for today. Report to me when you're dressed."

"Yes, sir."

"Dismissed."

I take the security pass off my arm, and hand it to the Commander. I pick up my helmet, and walk as fast as I can to the changing area. I pull my crate out from the stack, and make no effort to be quiet as I pull out my fatigues and pack my armour, helmet, and gun away. When I'm dressed, with my bootlaces tied, I sit for a moment with my head in my hands. I'm still angry, but the fight has gone out of me. I want to curl up in a corner and close my eyes. I want to talk to Charlie.

The Commander gives me the torturous task of tidying the marquee, cleaning the tables, and sweeping the floor. I stay as far away from Jackson as I can, and every time I look up I see Saunders watching me. He looks ready to burst into tears, and the only thing I can do is ignore him in case the same thing happens to me.

When the cleaning is done, the Commander sends me to the security gate to pick up trays, bowls, cups, and spoons for the evening meal. I push them to the marquee on a trolley and lay them out on the serving table, ready for the caterers to set up their food.

The music and cheering reach a peak of volume, and then the sound drops away. The concert is over, and the crowd will be filing out of the arena and heading for home. The catering staff arrive and I help them to move their equipment to the table. Jackson is directing the recruits to their new patrol areas.

The first of the arena patrols arrives back in the marquee, high-fiving each other and celebrating the end of their first assignment. It takes another hour for the last of the car park and street patrols to gather, but eventually we're all here, and the food is ready to be served. The Commander puts me on the catering team, and I'm handing out bread rolls and chocolate bars as the rest of the recruits pick up their food and sit down to eat. Dan gives me a confused look as I put food on his tray – I'm the only person in uniform behind the catering table. He starts to ask me something, but I cut him off with a shake of my head and offer bread and chocolate to the next recruit in line. I don't trust myself to speak without making a scene.

The Commander is the last person in the queue, and when I've served him, he tells me to fetch my own meal and sit with everyone else. I find a seat in the far corner of the marquee, and ignore everyone else at the table while I eat. Two or three people try to engage me in conversation, but they soon realise that I'm not going to join in, so they carry on without me.

After dinner, the Commander stands up and congratulates us on a successful first patrol. He's happy with how we've behaved and interacted with the public, and he passes on the thanks of the concert organisers.

"You've done a good thing today, recruits. You've given people confidence to come out of their homes, to defy the rebels, and to enjoy themselves. You've been excellent ambassadors for your government, and you've given the TV stations some great footage to show off your service. Give yourselves a cheer!"

The marquee erupts with cheering and whooping. Recruits are banging their fists on the tables and stamping their feet on the floor. The Commander holds up his hands for quiet.

"Tomorrow, you'll all have the day off. Breakfast is at eight, and the training run is cancelled. You'll have the run of the base. Enjoy yourselves – you've earned it!"

The next cheer is even louder.

*****

We collect our armour crates and load them back under the bus in the floodlit car park. We climb on board, and I'm hoping to sit alone, but Dan finds me, and takes the seat next to me.

"You OK, Bex?"

I shake my head. He makes a show of looking me up and down.

"You seem OK. No limbs hanging off. No bleeding. Wait …" He makes me lean forward so he can pretend to inspect my back. "Nope. Nothing. You're completely fine!"

In spite of myself, he's making me smile.

"We're OK, Bex," he says, more seriously, "we got through it. They didn't target us. We're safe."

I nod. He puts his arm round me, and I fall asleep, my head against his shoulder.

*****

The day before Margie disappeared, we argued. She was so sure that the terrorists were right, and Dan was so sure that the government was protecting us. I think she had already decided to leave.

We'd completed our homework tasks, and Dan pulled a pack of cards from his pocket, but it stayed, untouched on the table. The conversation was heated, and no one was in the mood for a game.

"How can you write that? How can you scribble that down like a good, obedient child while the government is bulldozing our freedom?"

Dan had written an essay on the state of emergency, and justified the government's actions with a list of ter-

rorist attacks and casualty numbers. Margie was furious, but so was Dan.

"What's the point of freedom if you're too scared to use it?" Margie tried to respond, but Dan shouted over her. "What's the point of freedom if you're dead, Margie? What good is freedom to the people blown up in the Crossrail tunnel? We need to survive this, and we need to get out the other side, and enjoy our freedom again, without fear."

Margie sat up straight in her chair, trying to stay calm.

"What's the point of surviving if you don't have the right to make your own decisions, Dan? What's the point of sitting still and letting the government march all over us, if all we get at the end is institutionalised slavery?"

Dan laughed. "You really do have an amazing imagination, don't you? You really think that at the end of this the government won't throw a big party and hold an election and give us back our votes? They'll probably give us a new Bank Holiday and a set of commemorative stamps, too." He holds up his fingers in air quotes. "'Victory Day'. Fireworks. Street parties. Politicians kissing babies."

Margie let out a single, sharp laugh.

"This is all for the good, Margie. They're making sure that there is a country for us to wake up in, and go to work in, and go to school in when the terrorists are defeated. They're keeping us safe. Short-term hardship for long-term gain." He shrugged.

"And what's the end game? When will your benevolent government decide that the emergency is over? What has to happen to make them grant you your freedom again?"

"Beat the terrorists. Parade every last one of them on TV in chains. Lock them up. When we can go out without *fear of another bombing, their job is done. I'll have my vote back, thank you."*

"And your fireworks", I said, just to break the tension. I didn't know who to side with, but I didn't want to see my friends fighting like this.

"And my fireworks!" Dan banged his fist on the table, laughing. "Exactly."

Margie pretended to think this over.

"So ... all the extra money going to the army, all the billions going to defence contractors for guns and equipment to fight these terrorists. The army and the owners of the defence companies – they're just going to say 'OK, have your cash back. I don't need it any more.' They won't put up a fight if the government declares that the terrorists have been defeated?"

"I'm sure the government will honour their contracts. I'm sure they won't just switch off the money tap. The gun manufacturers know that the fight can't go on forever. But while it does – yes, they should be paid, and they should employ people, and they should be proud to be protecting the rest of us."

"And you don't think the weapons manufacturers might have friends in the government? Might have reasons to pay people off to keep the fight going, and the money rolling in?"

Dan leaned back in his chair and waved his hand, dismissively. "Oh, come on. Now you're just being paranoid. Bribing the government to keep fighting the baddies? That's childish."

I listened to the two of them, to their wildly different points of view, and I couldn't decide who was right. My own essay had weighed up the arguments, and pointed out the reasons for the attacks, but also the reasons for the state of emergency. I could see that we needed to defend ourselves, but I could also see that the government's reaction could provoke more attacks.

"Don't you think there's a balance to be struck here? Don't you think that the government could be less extreme, and maybe there would be fewer attacks?"

"Yes! Exactly, Bex." Margie glanced at me, then turned back to Dan. "Bex gets it."

I shook my head – I hadn't intended to argue on Margie's side. Or on Dan's. I just wanted some balance in the discussion.

"No! Neither of you gets it! People who use bombs on civilians only understand one language, and that's the language of force. They need a bigger, scarier force, fighting on the side of the civilians, to scare them off, and make them stop. We've got that. That's what's happening."

"Fine, Dan. If you're so convinced that the government is doing the right thing – if you're so married to their vote-stealing, democracy-killing civil war – then why don't you enlist?"

She stood up, so fast that her chair tipped backwards onto the floor, picked up her books from the table and marched out of the room, leaving the door swinging open behind her.

Dan looked as if she'd punched him. We'd never truly fallen out over an argument before. He stared after her, and then said, in a small voice, "Because I want to be a doctor. I want to stay at school."

I couldn't think of anything to say. Dan picked up his pack of cards and put it back in his pocket. We sat in silence for a while before heading off to our dormitories.

That was the last time we saw Margie. At our history lesson the next day, we heard that Dr Richards had left as well.

Camp

"They've caught someone trying to break into the camp." Dan crashes his breakfast tray onto the table and sits down opposite me to eat. "They're saying it's a terrorist, scouting us out for an attack."

"Seriously?"

"For real. Really ballsy, too. They tried to walk right through the gates next to a delivery truck that was driving in last night. Got caught, though." Dan shrugs, and digs his fork into his scrambled egg.

"Are they still in the camp?"

He nods. "Rumour is, they're in the empty dorm, under guard. I think the Commander's wondering who else might turn up if we keep them here. Use them as bait."

I eat in silence, thinking. I finish my breakfast and stand up. Dan looks up, surprised. "See you later?"

"Yeah." I manage a smile, slide my tray into the rack by the door, and head back to my dorm room.

It's an overcast morning. Through the windows I can see lights in the empty dorm building, and soldiers at the doors. I pause to watch, as one of the soldiers opens the front door, and a member of the camp staff walks out, down the steps, carrying an empty meal tray.

My dorm is empty. Everyone is determined to enjoy their day off, and the opportunity for a leisurely breakfast is keeping most people in the dining room, enjoying the lack of schedule. I sit down on my bunk and think.

What are the terrorists doing here? We're just the crowd control, not the army. They must be planning something big.

I need to talk to the prisoner. I need to know if they know where Margie is, and Dr Richards. What they're doing. Why Margie left.

I need a plan. I need to talk to Charlie.

*****

I throw on a sweater, and take a walk across the camp to the back door of the kitchen. I knock, and someone I don't recognise opens the door. She looks at me, and then turns away into the kitchen area.

"Charlie! It's your little lost puppy!"

She flashes me an unkind grin, and lets the door close on me.

Seconds later, Charlie opens the door, slips out and closes it behind her.

"Bex. What's up?"

"Have you heard …"

She puts her finger to her lips, grabs my elbow, and pulls me away from the door. We walk away from the kitchen to the furthest picnic bench, where she climbs up to sit on the table, and pats the space beside her.

"The prisoner? Yes. I figured you'd be interested."

"Have you seen …"

"No. But they're in the empty dorm, under guard."

"I need to get inside."

"I thought you were going to say that. Leave it with me. Come back before lunch – I might have a job for you to do."

"Thanks, Charlie."

She stays sitting on the table, looking out at the morning sky.

"So how was your first patrol?"

"It was … it was fine."

She turns to look at me.

"Fine? That's all?"

"Nothing happened. There was nothing for us to do, but there were cameras everywhere. We were on show. Front-line dolls."

"I'm sure that's not true. You made a difference. You made people feel better about going out and having fun."

"There was a photographer. He took photos of us. It wasn't about our training – no one cared how quickly we could run an assault course or fire a gun. They just wanted to see us in our armour. We're the pretty faces of public security." I'm getting angry again, and I know I'll start crying if I don't change the subject. "How was your day in the empty camp?"

"More exciting than yours, by the sound of it. We had an NBC drill."

I must look confused.

"Nuclear-biological-chemical? Those stupid white suits and gas masks? They sounded the alarm and dumped a load of NBC suits in our common room. We had five minutes to grab a suit and put it on over our uniforms, and then two buses turned up and they evacuated the site. We spent half the day in a church hall, with someone else making the tea and coffee for a change. They brought us home in time for dinner, which was late because we hadn't been here to cook it. Waste of a day, if you ask me. And no cameras here. We're not glamorous like you." She smiles and winks at me, then glances at the kitchen door over my shoulder.

"I need to get back to work. You lot have left me a pile of washing up, and it needs to get done in time for lunch." She steps down from the table. "Enjoy your day off – but don't get used to it. You'll be back to training tomorrow."

"Thanks, Charlie," I say, and I manage a smile.

I sit on the table for a while longer, thinking about the prisoner, and what they might be able to tell me. If Charlie can get me inside, or carry messages to the dorm, I might be able to find out where the rebels are – where Margie is. Whether she's in any danger.

I jump off the table and walk back to the dining room to look for Dan.

Prisoner

We spend the morning playing cards, talking about our lives before conscription, and reading magazines that someone has managed to persuade the camp staff to share with us. I'm sitting with Dan, Amy, Saunders, and Jake, but other recruits join us for games and conversations. It's amazing to spend time with these people when we're not running or training, or exhausted at meal times. Saunders is sketching again, and recruits I've never spoken to are coming over and asking him to draw them. He's thrilled to be the centre of attention.

Before lunch, I excuse myself from the next game of cards, and walk back to the kitchen door. I knock, and Charlie answers, glances around and lets me in. She hands me a kitchen staff uniform.

"Get changed", she whispers.

I swap my fatigues for an outfit that looks like white scrubs, with a dark blue tabard. She hides my clothes in her locker, and heads to the kitchen to fetch the meal tray.

I straighten my tabard, and adjust the neckline of the tunic underneath. There's a mirror on the wall, and I check my appearance, making sure that nothing stands out. At the last minute I decide that my hair is untidy. I take the clip out, roll the hair into a smart up-do, and clip it into place.

Charlie returns, hands me the tray, and opens the door for me. I step out, carrying the prisoner's meal.

"Walk to the door. Look confident. The guard will let you in. Take the tray to the prisoner's room, and wait while they eat. You should be able to ask a couple of questions without making anyone suspicious. Keep your voice down, and don't give the welfare worker anything to talk about. When they're done, come straight back here with the empty tray." She talks quietly, and keeps looking over my shoulder for anyone who might recognise me.

The walk to the empty dorm seems impossibly long. I walk briskly but carefully, watching the tray, careful not to spill anything. The prisoner is being treated well – they have a good helping of food, some fresh fruit, a bottle of water. No chocolate, though. And no knife or fork. There's not much damage they can do with a spoon.

The soldier on guard duty glances quickly at me before opening the door. The uniform is what he is expecting to see, and he doesn't notice that I'm not a member of the kitchen staff.

I'm inside. I cross the hall, and push open the door to the corridor. Another member of camp staff sits on a chair outside a door, halfway down. The space is dimly lit, but the light is on in what I assume is the prisoner's room. I nod to the staff member, but she's reading a dog-eared magazine, and waves me through without looking up. According to her name tag, her name is Harriet.

I step into the prisoner's room, tightening my grip on the tray. I don't know what I'm going to find inside. I'm not sure what I'm expecting to see, but it isn't this.

This is Margie.

She's been beaten up. Her hair is shorter and shaggy, and her clothes (camouflage fatigues and a T-shirt, like mine) are muddy. She's got a split lip and a graze above her eye. She's sitting at a small table, waiting.

She looks up, and her eyes widen. "Oh my god!"

I shush her, quickly, glancing back towards the door.

I step forward, and put the tray down in front of her. Holding my finger to my lips, I pick up the bottle of water, loosen the lid, and throw it hard at the floor towards the door.

We both shout, wordlessly, as the bottle bursts and water sprays out into the corridor, and then I'm down on my knees, apologising, trying to rescue the bottle.

Harriet jumps to her feet and stands, looming in the doorway.

"I'm so sorry!" I say, looking lost, kneeling on the wet floor. "I – I dropped it."

I do my best to look desperate.

"Would you mind? The prisoner needs water, and I'm supposed to stay here with the tray. Could you – would you – go to the kitchen for me?"

Harriet rolls her eyes, but it's obvious that she's been sitting here for hours, and the opportunity to take a break is too tempting. She sighs loudly, and walks away down the corridor. I make myself take a calming breath. We're safe, for now.

I pick up the bottle, and turn back to Margie. We both speak at once.

"What are you –"

"Why are you –"

"Oh, god, Bex!" And she stands up and hugs me. I hug her back. I can't believe she's here.

"They thought I could sneak into camp – pose as one of you. They even kitted me out like a recruit, but it didn't work as well as they'd hoped." She waves her hands at her muddy outfit.

"We only have a few minutes. What are you doing here? Is it true that you're scouting for an attack?"

She looks at me as if I've pulled a gun on her. "What? No!"

"Then why –"

"I'm here to get to you lot. I'm here to warn you."

"Warn us? About what? What are you – wait. This *is* about an attack." I feel a flash of anger. Margie knows about a terrorist plot, and she's here to get us out of the way. "Margie, what's the target? What are you aiming for? This is a quiet town – what damage could you possibly do?"

She's shaking her head. I glance over my shoulder. We don't have time for this.

"Tell me what you know!" I'm shouting, even though I know I should be quiet. I'm angry, and I'm frightened, and I don't have time for games.

"Bex! Bex. Just … shut up and listen." I put the crushed bottle on the table – I've been twisting it in my hands, but I hadn't noticed – and I nod. "OK. Thank you."

She takes a deep breath.

"The attack has already happened."

I shake my head. "What do you mean?"

"The attack is done. Over."

"Then why are you here?"

"To tell someone – and thank god it's you, Bex – to let someone know that this wasn't us."

I start to interrupt, but I can't find the words. I'm trying to understand what she's telling me.

"There's been an attack, Bex. A big one. But we didn't do it. You did."

I try to protest, but she cuts me off. "Not you, personally. The government. Your commanders. Your side. We don't know what they've done, but it's big. We had people in town, looking for targets, but we haven't heard from them since yesterday. We've sent scouts in, but there's no one left. There's nothing … Bex – they've killed the town."

There are tears in her eyes, but I know she's wrong. I know she's lying. She has to be.

The door at the end of the corridor slams, and we're out of time. I'm shaking my head, and I'm trying to ignore the tears building in my eyes.

"You're wrong. You're wrong."

"Bex," she whispers, urgently, "Just go and see. OK? Just go into town and see for yourself. I promise I'm telling the truth."

I stare at her.

Harriet arrives at the door, holding out a bottle of water. I nod thanks, and take the bottle, trying to hide any trace of my anger. I place it carefully on the table, and make myself walk away, out into the corridor. I stand, eyes fixed on a point on the opposite wall, while Margie eats her meal. She calls me back to take the tray, and as I reach to pick it up she grabs my hand.

"Promise me, Bex. Promise me you'll go."

I take the tray, pull out of her grasp, and leave.

*****

I hurry back to the kitchen and knock on the door. Charlie lets me in, takes the tray, and pulls my clothes from her locker. I change back into my fatigues and put my hair back in my usual rough pony tail. Charlie takes the tray to the kitchen and comes back for the uniform.

"Nice move with the water bottle," she whispers as she opens the laundry bin and dumps the kitchen scrubs inside. "Did you get your answers?"

My mind is racing, trying to understand what Margie told me. I need to check her story.

"I think so." I try to focus on Charlie. "Thank you for your help."

"You're welcome. Now make it count."

I nod. "I will." I'm already hatching a plan.

Outside

I'm back in the dining room in time for lunch. The kitchen staff have laid out bread and sandwich fillings, and left us to make our own meals. As I walk in, Dan is standing at the table with Amy and Saunders, intoning sacrificial words over a banana. Suddenly, this place doesn't seem so far from school, and from our real lives. I can't stop the smile spreading across my face.

Over sandwiches, prepared under Dan's watchful and exacting eye, and stuffed with fillings, we discuss the luxury of having a day off. We tell each other what we would do this afternoon if we were allowed to leave the base. We fantasise about trips to the cinema, or going to a concert as a member of the audience, or just going shopping.

When we've stacked our trays onto the kitchen racks, Dan pulls a pack of cards from his back pocket, and asks what we'd like to play. I tell them that I'm going to my bunk for a rest, and leave them to choose a game without me.

"You OK, Bex?" Dan looks concerned.

"Ask me later." I leave before I'm tempted to say anything else.

Back in my dorm room, I check that the other bunks are empty. I close the door, pull out my armour crate, and quickly change into the base layers. I tie my boots, and clip on my armour panels, making sure that the air canister, contamination panel, and radio modules are clipped into place. If there are cameras in town, I need to look official. If anyone is watching the training field, I need to look as if I am putting myself through a training run in full armour. I pick up my helmet and gun, kick the crate back under my bunk, and head out of the building.

Outside, I attach my helmet, and clip my gun to the back of my armour. I take a look around the field, and start to jog around the perimeter. There are a few recruits running the assault course, and another group running like me, but without armour. I can't see any senior recruits, and all the activity I can see is informal – groups of recruits passing the time with the equipment we have on the base. I jog once around the field, waving at the other recruits as I pass them. On my second lap, they wave back. By my third, they're ignoring me. I run another lap while I decide whether I am brave enough to leave the base. I'm breaking a sweat, but it is mostly the thought of what I am about to do, and what would happen if anyone caught me.

I know I can't leave through the main gate. We don't have permission to go outside the fence, and I know that the guards don't make exceptions – even for injured recruits in the rain. My only option is to go under the fence. I look out for the broken section of fence as I run, and reassure myself that it is completely hidden by the trees in the corner of the field. On my fifth lap, I run into the trees, crouch down next to the fence, unclip my gun and crawl underneath before I can think about it.

I'm outside the fence. I clip my gun to my back, check the field behind me for any sign that I've been seen leaving, and then turn and run deeper into the woods. I'm terrified and thrilled at the same time. I'm doing something forbidden, and I'm getting away with it. I want to whoop and punch the air, but I need to concentrate on running. I don't want to trip, like Saunders.

I run through the woods towards the main road, tracing our morning runs in reverse, wondering what Margie meant about the attack. She said that it had already happened. She said she was here to warn us. I'm trying to understand what she was telling me, but I can't make sense of it.

Before long, I'm out of the woods, and running along the bypass – but something's wrong. It's much too quiet.

I haven't seen a single car. I slow down, looking for traffic or people. Someone taking a walk. Someone driving to the shops.

But there's no one here.

I stop, and step into the road. I turn around, and look up and down the carriageway, but there are no cars – no vehicles at all. The hairs on the back of my neck are standing up. This is wrong.

I step back onto the pavement and start to run again, faster this time. I need to get into town. I need to see people and traffic, and reassure myself that everything is normal. I'm breathing heavily and I can feel the sweat, cold against my back, as I reach the industrial estate.

Town

I'm walking into town, along the busy road I've come to know, but the buildings that should be here are gone. The road is blocked with cars, all empty, all silent. The trees are ragged shards of splintered wood. The road surface is split with deep cracks.

I can't take in what I'm seeing. This is our town – it should be full of people. People driving, people walking, people carrying shopping and walking dogs and bringing their children home from school. I don't know where the people are.

Along the road, between the cars, I see pieces of people's lives. There's a handbag, dropped next to a car. A brightly coloured raincoat on the grass verge. A pink teddy bear. A single red glove.

I keep walking, past the skeletons of buildings. Shops, offices, factories, schools; all demolished. Here and there a steel frame breaks the skyline, or the corner of a brick wall. I hold my gun more tightly. I'm searching for any sign of life, or any clue as to what happened here.

All I can think is that the terrorists must hate us, to do something like this. To attack ordinary people, far from any government buildings. To destroy everything in town.

And suddenly, I can't breathe. I'm on my knees at the side of the road, clawing at my helmet, twisting it out of the neck seal on my suit, taking great gasps of air as I try to calm down and think clearly. Who did this? Why would they attack here? Where are all the people?

The silence is terrifying. I can hear gusts of wind whistling through the remains of the buildings, and something creaking on the other side of the road. With my helmet off, this feels way too real.

There's a faint chemical scent in the air. I can't place it, but it doesn't smell fresh or natural. I check my contamination panel and it's a pale shade of pink in the Chemical zone. I take a few more deep breaths and put my helmet back on, sealing myself off from the cold reality.

I pull myself to my feet, force myself to keep walking.

More cars. More buildings. More splinters of trees.

And then I see movement, up ahead. Figures in suits like mine, but black all over. Their black visors are closed, and the grey daylight reflects from their helmets as they crouch down in a parking lot to inspect something on the ground.

I shouldn't be here. I can't risk being seen. There's a third figure, walking round the building beside them, gun cradled across its body. It stops near the crouching suits and stands guard, gaze sweeping up and down the road as they work. I freeze. I can't afford to be seen.

Slowly, I crouch down and crawl into the road, between the cars, silent as I can be. I sit with my back against the wheel of a grey family car, gun across my knees, out of sight, and wait.

Under the car next to me, there's a shoe, the kind a woman might wear to work in an office. Slip-on – hard to run in, and easy to lose. I look more closely at the car, and realise that the front door is open, just a crack. Someone has opened it, and not stopped to close it. They've not stopped to pick up the shoe, either. Or the handbag. Or the teddy bear.

Did the people in the cars get out and run away? Or were they dragged from their cars while they were trying to drive? A little further ahead along the road, the cars are not in straight lines any more. They're slewed across the road, diagonal and messy, like a bad accident. There's a car half up on the verge, near the parking lot where the people in suits are working. The drivers were trying to avoid something, to get away from something.

My suit radio crackles to life, and I start, and nearly drop my gun. A local broadcast from somewhere in town.

"All units East, all units East: report."

So these are government troops. I'll be in trouble if they find me, but I won't be a prisoner. We're on the same side. I mute my microphone, hold my breath, and wait to see who responds.

"Unit Five, condition green. Over."

"HQ to Unit Five: understood. Over."

"Unit Three, condition green. Over."

"HQ to Unit Three: understood. Over."

I risk a glance over the cars to the parking lot. The guard taps his wrist to activate his radio, and I hear his voice.

"Unit Two, condition amber. Code 17 in location 128. Proceeding as ordered. Over."

"HQ to Unit Two: understood. Do you require back-up? Over."

"Negative, HQ. This is routine. Object will be ready for pickup in 5 minutes. Over."

"HQ to Unit Two: acknowledged. Pickup authorised. Continue to your next retrieval location. HQ out."

That means more soldiers heading this way. I need to disappear.

Two cars ahead of me on the road is an SUV, with tall wheel arches and the ground clearance to match. If I can get under there, I'll be out of sight to anyone walking along the road.

I swing my gun into its clips on my back, and lie face-down in the road. I start to crawl, low against the pavement, on my elbows and knees. Past the car I have been sitting against, past the gap between the car opposite and the car in front. I'm being as quiet as I can, but it's hard to tell how much noise I'm making in the silence.

The radio beeps in my ear, and I lie still in the road.

"Unit Two to HQ: we're done here. Heading out to location 129. Object is ready for retrieval at location 128. Over."

"HQ to Unit Two: good work, ladies and gents. Keep it up. HQ Out."

The people in the parking lot are moving on. I need to be under that SUV. I start to crawl again, as fast as I dare.

I'm getting closer to the parking lot. I catch sight of the object, a grey cylinder with red markings, through the gap under the car next to me. The people in the suits are standing near it. I can see their boots and gloves as they collect up their equipment and pack it into black cases.

Very slowly, I crawl along the road, and silently thank my luck when I notice that the car next to me has run into the car in front, closing the gap and keeping me out of sight while I crawl to the SUV. I keep glancing at the object and the soldiers, glimpsing them through the gaps under the cars. I'm almost at the SUV, trying to avoid the broken glass and plastic in the road from the car crash next to me. I crawl past the rear wheel, just as the soldiers pick up their cases and start to walk towards the road. Towards me.

I reach the SUV, and start to roll underneath. My gun catches on the door, and I'm stuck in the road. I can't see the boots, but I know they're getting closer. I roll back, into the road, my heartbeat loud in my ears. I grab my gun, tear off my helmet, and roll under the vehicle. Freeze.

I can hear footsteps, loud on the pavement, and the small sounds that armour makes as you walk. I hold my breath. I can hear muffled voices – they must be using their radios to talk to each other on a private channel. I hear laughter, and someone breaks stride, scuffing their feet on the ground.

My lungs are burning. My limbs are aching. My hands are wrapped tightly around my helmet and gun. I will myself to stay still.

And then the boots are there, in the road, next to me. Three soldiers. They've seen me. They must have seen me. They stop, and someone spins on the spot, a dance move, absurd in this place of silence. More laughter, and the boots move on, out of sight.

It takes me a moment to believe that I am safe, to breathe again, to relax. My heart is hammering, and I'm shaking, but I'm still here. I lie still for a minute or two to give the soldiers time to move away.

And then I realise what the object is. It should be impossible, it shouldn't be here, but the more I think about it, the more I'm sure. That's a government weapon.

I think about our weapons training video. Grey cylinder. Red markings. It's a City Killer.

There will be many of them, in a grid across the town. They will have been dropped, by drone, into accurate positions, and activated remotely. Individually, they wouldn't do much damage, but together? In a network, they work together to trigger an electro-magnetic pulse. That knocks out anything electrical: cars, phones, radios, lights – anything that runs on electricity. Then they coordinate to produce a ground tremor, faint at first, but escalating until buildings fall apart, trees shake themselves to pieces, and people fall. The drones fly back into range and watch the process, and when the destruction is sufficient, the remote operators shut off the devices. Job done.

If you want to make sure there are no survivors, you add a chemical element. Gas canisters that open when the shaking stops. I look down at my contamination panel – the colour is getting darker. Nowhere near the danger point yet, but there are residual chemicals in the air.

I'm missing something. The terrorists don't have these weapons – they're far too advanced. Maybe I was wrong. Maybe I was mistaken about what I saw.

I need to see the object up close.

Danger

Keeping very still, I hold my breath and listen to the sounds around me. The soldiers have gone – far enough away that I can no longer hear their footsteps. I can hear the wind, whistling through the ruins. There's no other sound.

Very carefully, I slide myself out from under the SUV. I check behind and ahead of me on the road, then sit up and put my helmet on, twisting it back onto my suit. Gripping my gun tightly, I push up into a crouch, and raise my head so I can see over the cars to the object.

No one around. I duck back down, check my surroundings again, then stand. Bent low to stay out of sight, I walk round the crashed cars in front of me and into the parking lot.

The object is a grey metallic cylinder, about waist-height, and as wide as my shoulders. It has a domed top, which makes it look like a missile, waiting for launch. But this thing has been launched. It's dropped its payload. The soldiers I saw were making sure of that. This is the mechanism for the EMP and the tremors, with an empty chemical tank, nothing more.

I walk around the object. The red markings on its side confirm my suspicions – this is a government weapon. The codes relate to its function, but also its deployment commands. There's a computer-readable code printed on the side. I try scanning it with my glove.

My radio announces, loudly, the unit and commander of the force that activated this weapon, but I don't believe what I am hearing. That can't be right. I scan it again.

"Commander Holden, Special Weapons Unit, Emergency Armed Forces Act. 7866577B-12"

The Emergency Armed Forces Act.

The reason I'm here.

The government did this.

*****

I'm shaking. I'm shaking and I'm angry and I don't know how to understand what I'm seeing. I sit down, hard, on the cold ground. There are tears in my eyes, on my cheeks, running in hot streams down my neck and soaking the collar of my base layers.

I stare at the object. The government's weapon. My army's weapon, used on my town, and on innocent people. My people.

We're not the terrorists! We're not killing people and taking hostages and breaking this country. We're *fighting* the terrorists. We're protecting the people. We're guarding hospitals and schools and factories all over the country, making sure that life can continue, that the terrorists won't win.

Aren't we?

What happened here?

What the *hell* happened?

My radio barks to life. The cleanup team is here. I can hear the sound of their vehicle approaching: time to move.

I stand up and look for somewhere to hide. At the back of the parking lot, away from the road, are the remains of a building. This used to be a row of shops, and there's a brick corner still standing, next to an empty doorway. I jog over to the door, gun raised, and step through into the shadow of the wall. I crouch down, and make sure no one outside can see me.

The frame of the roof, and the wooden beams that supported the second floor, are jumbled on top of the pile of bricks behind me. If anyone comes looking for me, I'm trapped, but I'm counting on them not being here to explore.

The noise of their recovery vehicle turns to a roar in the quiet street as they pull out from a side road and drive along the verge, driving into the cars and pushing them out of the way. There's a crashing sound and a screaming of metal dragging against metal.

A pickup truck with oversized wheels hurls itself into the parking lot and stops next to the weapon. There's a crack in the brickwork in front of me, and I use it to watch the pickup team jump from the truck, scan the weapon, and load it onto the back of the vehicle. I expect them to jump back in and drive away, but instead they stand around, stretching and rolling their shoulders, talking on a private channel.

One of them checks his contamination panel, shrugs, and takes off his helmet. He takes a deep breath, and grins. The others join him – helmets off, ration packs out. They're taking a meal break, here.

And then I see their faces clearly. It's Jackson and Ketty, and another of the Senior Recruits, laughing and eating ration bars as if this is all a joke. The bruises on my ribs are still fresh, and I know they mustn't find me here. I might not be so lucky this time.

Jackson laughs, and points to something on the ground in front of my hiding place. For a chilling moment I think he's pointing at me, but the others turn and laugh, and I'm still hidden. He jogs across to my hiding place and stands with his back to the wall, blocking my view of the others. He's so close – I mustn't move. I mustn't make a sound. He picks something up from the ground, and jogs back to the truck.

My legs are cramping, and I'm regretting not finding a more comfortable hiding place. I cannot move – I cannot give myself away. I've already overstayed my time in town, and I'll miss roll call if I don't head back soon.

I'm starting to regret this whole adventure. I had to come and see for myself, but what good has it done me? I've only earned myself another beating and a punishment detail. I check my contamination panel. Darker than before.

It's a lipstick. They've picked up a lipstick from the ground in front of me, and now they're trying to catch each other's suits with it, shouting and dodging the tiny weapon. Eventually, Ketty gets hold of it, and convinces the others to stand still. She holds their heads steady, and draws war paint on their faces. Three stripes from hairline to chin for Jackson, running over his closed eyes. Angled stripes on the cheekbones for the other man, and one stripe for her, splitting her face in two from forehead to neck. Laughing, she tosses the lipstick away, and climbs back into the truck.

I watch the lipstick roll across the pavement and out of sight.

The truck engine starts. All three put their helmets on, and settle into their seats. Ketty guns the engine and angles the truck across the road, ploughing the cars out of the way as she goes. The noise is like pain, and I know she's laughing.

After

Dinner is tight, but I make it. I walk back to camp through the trees, keeping out of sight for as long as possible, sticking to the shadows. I slip back in under the fence, and start jogging round the perimeter, as if I've been running circuits of the field all afternoon. At the dormitory, I break away from the fence and let myself in through the back door, stripping off my helmet and gloves as I hurry along the corridor.

I have time to drop my armour and gun into the crate, throw my fatigues on over my base layers, and head towards the hall. The meal bell rings as I reach the doorway, and I'm in line with everyone else when Commander Bracken and Robin the clipboard carrier walk through the front door for the evening briefing. For a moment, I wonder where the Senior Recruits are, but then I experience a vivid flash of memory: Ketty ploughing her vehicle through the lines of cars. I close my eyes and shake my head with the realisation that everything that has happened this afternoon, everything I saw out there, was real.

My knees start to give way, and I'm fighting to stay standing. I put my hand on the edge of a table to support my weight. Someone is calling my name, and I realise that I'm at the front of the queue. Someone behind me pushes me gently forwards, and I manage to take a tray and accept a bowl of food. I force myself to take a bottle of water from the table, and I turn round to look for a seat. Dan is on the far side of the room, waving me over. I start walking towards him. All the sound in the room seems very loud and very distant at the same time. I can't hear what anyone is saying, but everyone keeps talking at once. I take one step, and another, and keep going until I reach Dan's table. I put my tray down, pull out a chair, and sit.

I can't even look at the food in front of me. I'm still trying to understand what happened to the people. I remember the contamination panel, and the City Killer. The gas. The cars. The woman's shoe. The teddy bear.

I put my head in my hands and close my eyes, tight.

Dan is saying something to me. He's crouching next to me on the floor, gently shaking my shoulder. I need to move. I need to get control of myself, and look as if I'm OK. I take a deep breath, and look up.

"Bex, seriously. What's the matter?"

"I'm OK," I mumble. "I'm OK." I shake his hand off my shoulder, sit up straight, and pull my chair in closer to the table. I make an effort to look around, and smile at the people next to me.

"I'm OK. Honestly." I pick up my fork, but I still can't force myself to eat. I poke my food while Dan goes back to his seat. Everyone is watching me. Dan looks at me with concern. He reaches across the table and takes my hand.

"Go and lie down, Bex," he says. "You look like you've seen a ghost."

I almost laugh, but it comes out as a sob. I will myself not to burst into tears; and nod.

"Yeah. I should go." I stand up to leave, and Dan hands me my water bottle. It's a small act of kindness, but it reminds me that even in a world where the people I work for – the people who kidnapped me and my friends – just destroyed a town full of civilians, someone still cares about me. I leave the room as the tears are welling up in my eyes, and my vision is blurry all the way back to my bunk. I pull off my fatigues and base layers, change into pyjamas and climb into my narrow bed. I pull the covers over my head and lie in silence, tears streaming onto my pillow.

What did Margie mean? Did the government really do this to the town? Is that why they emptied the camp –

so the gas wouldn't poison anyone here? Why Saunders came to Birmingham, even though he couldn't join us on patrol? Why the camp staff had an NBC drill?

And I realise that it wasn't a drill. They couldn't afford to have anyone at the camp while the City Killers were running. Anyone still here would have felt the vibrations, and been in danger from the gas. They needed to have no witnesses, so they took us all off site.

And then they killed the town.

I'm angry and I'm frightened. I've seen things that I shouldn't have seen. I know what my government has done, and I can't report it to anyone. I can't be the one person who knows. I can't stay here.

And then I remember that Margie knows, too. It's not safe for either of us here.

We need to leave.

Truth

In the morning I drag myself out of bed. I take a shower, and wash my face again with cold water to hide my puffy eyes. I get dressed and allow myself to follow the morning routine I've grown used to. Down the corridor to the dining room. Take a tray of food, sit down, make myself eat. Saunders sits down next to me, flips my mug the right way up and pours the coffee. He doesn't say anything, but eats his breakfast without comment. Dan joins us, and surrounded by quiet conversations, we eat in silence.

I'm thinking about how I'm going to make it through today without screaming, or telling someone what I saw in town. How I'm going to concentrate on training and not on the City Killers. How I'm going to get Margie out of here.

Commander Bracken strides in, followed by the Senior Recruits, and we all stand. The screeching of the chairs makes me cringe, and I close my eyes to block out the room around me.

"Recruits!"

"Sir!"

"Be seated." More screeching as we all pull our chairs in to the tables. His assistant walks in, and starts to switch on and set up the television on the far wall.

"This morning, we have bad news. Today will not be the training day you are expecting. There has been an attack."

There are whispers and murmurs from around the room. I sit very still, staring at my empty plate, gritting my teeth and digging my fingernails in to the palms of my hands. I don't want to hear what the Commander is going to say, and I don't want to react in front of everyone. I feel sick, and I feel as if someone has dropped a heavy bag on my shoulders. I want to scream. I want to tell him that I know what he's done – what *we* have done. It takes all my concentration to keep quiet, and listen to what I know is coming next.

"We will not be following our usual route on the training run. Leominster is sealed off. The terrorists have struck on our doorstep, and we are only just coming to understand the severity of the attack.

"In the coming days, it will be our duty to assist the army in whatever capacity they require. You are no longer recruits. You have graduated to armed auxiliaries. The army can now request your service at any time.

"This is an extremely serious attack. It demonstrates that the rebels are no longer a background threat to our way of life. They are well-armed and very dangerous. We don't know where they will attack next, but we will be on call to help prevent future incidents, and to assist if they attack again."

He nods to the assistant, who switches the television to the Public Information Network and turns up the sound. It's seven o'clock, and the news report is just beginning.

The newsreader breaks the story, and hands over to a camera crew on the ground. I know what the images are going to show, and I don't want to see it again, but I can't stop watching. The room is silent.

The reporter is walking along another road in town, but it looks the same as the places I saw yesterday. The buildings have crumbled. The roads are blocked by crashed vehicles and empty cars. There are more abandoned possessions littering the road and the pavements. The town is in ruins.

There are gasps from around me. I keep my jaw tight and my fists clenched. I'm trying hard not to cry again, but the anger and the horror is building up. I realise I'm shaking and I do my best to relax. I can't expose my knowledge.

The screen is showing drone footage of the town, and I see what I hadn't seen before. People have gathered in open spaces – in parks, in car parks – and it is there that they have fallen, killed by the effects of the gas. They must have been directed there. There must have been troops evacuating the buildings, the vehicles, the streets. The people followed them, when the shaking started. They believed that they would be safe, and instead the gas killed them.

I'm fighting the urge to vomit.

The report ends, and the newsreader returns.

"Breaking news: the Prime Minister has just announced a heightened state of National Emergency, and the introduction of Martial Law. In the light of such an audacious terrorist attack, she has placed the security of the country in the hands of the army. Parliament will be dissolved, until such time as these attacks can be stopped, and the democratic process can be safely reinstated ..."

The assistant hurries to turn the television off. Commander Bracken points at the blank screen.

"This is what we are dealing with now. A terrorist army that can wipe out thousands of people in an afternoon. Fighters who hate us, and hate what we stand for, so much that they are willing to do this."

I want to shout. I want to scream at him that this wasn't the terrorists. This was us! We did this! I'm shaking, I'm angry, and I need to calm down. I can't accuse the Commander. If Ketty and Jackson could beat me up for helping other recruits, what would they do to me if they found out where I went yesterday? That I spoke to the prisoner? That the prisoner is my friend?

What would they do to Margie, if they knew what she had told me? What will they do to Margie, now that they are blaming the terrorists, officially, on the news? She could be the terrorist figurehead they've been looking for. The front-line doll from the enemy. Will they put her on television, too? What will happen to her?

"You will return to your dorms, and you will pack your belongings. The army will request support from me today, and some of you will be relocated to assist with their clean-up and protection duties. Be ready to leave when you are called. Ensure that your armour and weapons are in working order, and report any faults immediately.

"This is it. This is the real thing. You've been trained, you can handle the fight. Go out and protect the people who need you. Things are going to change from now on. You're on the front line. Dismissed!"

And with the screeching of the chairs, all I can think is 'cannon fodder'.

*****

I walk back to my dorm room in a daze, following the rush of people. Inside, there are people packing their bags, people checking their weapons, and there are people sitting and standing with stunned expressions on their faces. I make myself pull my rucksack from my locker, and start pushing clothes and belongings into it. I'm not paying attention, but this way I'm not facing other people in the room. I'm trying to clear my head and think quickly.

I need to tell Dan.

It will be dangerous for him to know, but if I'm going to get myself and Margie away from here, I'm going to need help. I finish filling my rucksack, and throw it onto my bed. I pull out my armour crate and stack it next to my bag. Then I head out through the confusion of recruits packing and talking, and go to find Dan.

I find him outside his dorm room, trying to convince Saunders to concentrate on packing bags and checking armour. Saunders looks stunned, and clearly needs someone to help him focus, but I don't have time to babysit him. I grab Dan's elbow, and keep walking, dragging him along the corridor with me.

"Bex! What are you … what's going on?"

I shush him, and pull him to the end of the corridor, then out through the back door of the dorm. I close the door, and drop his elbow, then look around for anyone who might overhear, checking along both sides of the building. There's no one close by, and everyone I can see is in a hurry – packing equipment onto vehicles, carrying bags and crates. I turn back to Dan.

"We don't have much time."

"What's …" he begins, but I cut him off.

"There's something you need to know. And I'm really sorry, but once you know, you're going to be in danger here." He looks at me as if I'm speaking another language.

"The prisoner is Margie."

"She's … what? She's here?" He can't help leaning round the side of the building to look at the empty dorm.

"I spoke to her."

"You … how?"

I shake my head in frustration.

"Never mind. But you need to hear what she told me." He nods. "The attack in town? That wasn't the terrorists. That was the government."

He's shaking his head now.

"No. No way, Bex. Why would they do that? And you've only got Margie's word for it. She's been brainwashed by the terrorists."

I'm shaking my head at him.

"What? You can't trust her, Bex. She's only telling you what she's been told. And why would the government do that? It makes no sense."

"I went into town."

"You did *what*? When?"

"Yesterday, while you were playing cards. I went under the fence, and I went into town."

He's gaping at me. He grabs my elbow.

"Have you gone completely mad? Why did you do that?"

"The attack didn't happen last night. It happened while we were in Birmingham." He's shaking his head. "Margie told me. She knew about the attack before the news report. She told me it wasn't them."

"And you believed her?"

"I had to go and find out."

He drops my elbow and turns away.

"What did you find?"

"We did it. She was right. They used City Killers. The soldiers must have evacuated people from their cars and their houses when the earthquakes started, and gathered them in the parks. That's where they were when the gas was released. I didn't understand where all the people were yesterday, but the news report showed what happened to them."

He's shaking his head. "How do you know that it was us? How do you know that the terrorists haven't stolen a warehouse of City Killers? It doesn't make any sense."

"Ketty and Jackson were there."

"What?"

"I saw Ketty and Jackson. They were on the clean-up crew. They were picking up the City Killers and getting rid of the evidence. And there were government soldiers switching them off and checking they were safe for collection." There are tears in my eyes, and I'm so relieved to be sharing this with someone else, but I'm seeing everything again, and remembering the fear and the horror of what I saw.

"Wait – you're sure about this?"

I nod, and brush tears from my cheeks.

"They were having fun. They thought it was a laugh, clearing the weapons and driving into abandoned cars. I was hiding, and they were so close to finding me ..." I take a breath, trying to think this through. "I have to get out. I can't be here and know this. And we have to get Margie out, too."

Dan puts his arm around my shoulders. He thinks for a moment, then nods, slowly.

"Martial law. That's how they're justifying putting the army in charge. They're using the attack as an excuse to get rid of the civilian government."

He gives me a quick hug, and pulls open the back door.

"Let me finish packing, and check on Saunders. I'll find you in half an hour."

I hope we have half an hour.

Help

I hurry to the kitchen. I'm going to need help from Charlie again if I stand a chance of getting close to Margie. As I walk past the windows, I can see Commander Bracken addressing the kitchen staff. At the back door to the kitchen, I hesitate. I don't want to draw attention to myself by interrupting, but I need to talk to Charlie as soon as possible. My mind is racing – I'm trying to come up with a plan that keeps everyone out of trouble, and gets Margie out of the camp. The current state of confusion offers us the best chance to do this without being detected, so I need to act quickly. A camp uniform will get me into the dorm. I need a way of sneaking Margie out unnoticed, and I need a way out of the camp.

The door slams open and a group of staff members hurries out, carrying crates of water bottles and flasks, and heading for the vehicle parking area. I wait for them to disappear round the corner of the building, then tuck myself in through the slowly closing door. There's no one in the locker room, but as I glance down the corridor to the kitchen I find Charlie walking towards me with another crate of water. I step back, round the corner next to the lockers, and wait.

"What are you doing here, Bex?" Charlie asks as she places the crate on the floor next to the door. "I thought you were all getting ready to leave." She straightens up and looks at me. "What's wrong?"

"I need the uniform again."

She shakes her head.

"No, Bex. It's too dangerous." I open my mouth to protest, but she cuts me off. "We're all running round with urgent jobs to do. I have no idea what they're planning for the prisoner, but I don't want to get in the way. Not after what their friends have done."

"But they haven't done anything."

"What? What are you talking about? You've seen the news, right?"

I'm shaking my head, and fighting back tears again.

"They didn't do it, Charlie. We did."

She steps towards me, and pulls me past the lockers to the end of the room.

"Say that again."

"The terrorists didn't kill the town. We did. I saw the weapons they used, and I saw the government troops clearing them away. Your NBC drill? That wasn't a drill. That's when they killed everyone in town. That's why they sent us to Birmingham – so there was no one on site when it happened."

"But it happened last night."

"It didn't. It happened when we were all off site. I saw it yesterday, before any of the reporters arrived."

"You went into town?" I nod. "You're crazier than I realised … and braver. What were you thinking? What if you'd got caught?"

There are tears in my eyes, but I half sob, half laugh at this. Charlie puts her arm round my shoulders.

"You could still get caught. They'll lock you up, or worse, if they find out what you know."

I nod, fighting the tears.

"And Margie. Margie knows, too. And I've told Dan."

Charlie straightens up, shakes her head, comes to a decision.

"OK. We have to get you out. What do you need?"

Confusion

Dan and Saunders track me down in the corridor outside Dan's dorm room. Recruits are still packing, talking and shouting, or sitting on their own, trying to process what they've seen. We're in the middle of chaos, and this is our opportunity to act.

I explain my plan, and hand them bundles of clothing and a stack of brightly coloured empty crates. We split up, and return to our dorm rooms to change – I pull my base layers on, put the staff uniform on top, and stuff my fatigues into the top of my rucksack. I transfer my armour, helmet, gun, and rucksack into a bright green crate from the kitchen, and carry it out of the building. We meet up outside the back door.

Dan has recruited Amy and Jake. Dressed in fatigues instead of staff uniforms, and carrying their belongings in their rucksacks, we agree that they will be our distraction, and we'll pick them up on our way out. Amy takes my crate, and I leave the others and walk back to the kitchen.

Charlie is waiting at the back door. She hands me a bottle of water and a chocolate bar.

"See you at the gate." She winks, and jingles a set of vehicle keys that she pulls from her pocket and puts straight back. "Go and get her," she says, and opens the door.

I grasp her hand quickly, tightly, then let go and begin my walk to the empty dorm.

It's another long walk, past groups of camp staff carrying supplies to vehicles, and Senior Recruits moving equipment. I'm fighting to stay calm. At the door, I show the snack and the bottle. The guard waves me through, and I cross the dining area towards the corridor.

Halfway across the room, I hear voices from the corridor. Batman and Robin, talking to … Ketty and Jackson? I look around for somewhere to hide.

Crouched under a table, I watch them walk across the dining room and leave the building. My heart is hammering, and I am starting to realise how dangerous this plan could be.

I stand up, and make my way towards Margie's room. I'm trying to look confident, but inside I'm terrified.

Outside the room, another member of staff is sitting, working on a newspaper crossword. I force a bright smile and hold up the chocolate and the water bottle.

"For the prisoner," I announce. He nods. "Do you want to take a break? I'll sit with her while she eats, if you like." I have no idea what he's been told about staying close to the room, but I'm hoping that he'll be as happy to take a break as Harriet was.

"Sure. Thanks. Just … don't lose her." He grins, puts his newspaper on the chair, and walks down the corridor to the dining room. As soon as he is out of sight, I run to the far end of the building and unlock the back door. I leave it cracked open, and run back to Margie's room.

She's lying on the bunk in the corner, bruises on her arms. She has a graze on her forehead, the beginnings of a black eye, and another cut on her lip. That's why Ketty and Jackson were here. Commander Bracken's go-to thugs. I feel sick at the thought of them beating my friend.

"Margie! Margie, it's me." She stirs, and looks at me, one eye swollen almost shut.

"Bex?"

"You need to get up. Sit up. Let me help you."

She looks confused, but she eases herself up until she's sitting on the edge of the bed. There's a sound from the corridor, and Saunders, already dressed in white, puts his head round the door. He walks quietly into the room, and holds out another camp staff uniform.

"Margie, you need to put these on. Stand up." Saunders and I help her to stand, and then Saunders retreats to the corridor while I help Margie out of her dirty T-shirt and trousers, and into the white scrubs. There's a pair of lightweight canvas shoes under her bed, which I help her to put on and lace up.

"We have to leave now. We're going to help you, but you need to walk. Can you walk for me?"

She nods, and I pull her arm round my shoulder and help her towards the door. In the corridor, Saunders, still limping himself, takes her other arm, and we half walk, half carry her to the back door.

Outside, Dan is waiting with our belongings in kitchen crates. He looks uncomfortable, dressed like me in white kitchen scrubs. I can hear Jake and Amy talking to the guard, round the corner of the building. They've distracted him for this long with questions about working for the army, but the conversation can't last much longer. We need to start moving.

I hand the chocolate bar and water bottle to Margie, pull her hair forward to cover her black eye, and check that she can walk on her own. Dan, Saunders, and I lift a crate each, and make sure that the armour is invisible inside. We set off across the field, walking purposefully, but not quickly enough to attract attention. Margie and Saunders, both limping, do their best to keep up, and I slow down to make sure no one is left behind.

We walk between knots of recruits, discussing their excitement about working for the army; kitchen staff, carrying crates like ours to vehicles in the parking area; and Senior Recruits, stacking equipment into piles and checking items off on their clipboards. Margie keeps her head down, letting her hair fall forward to hide her face.

With our camp staff uniforms, we are invisible in all the activity.

As we reach the parking area, Amy and Jake catch up with us and jog past, still in their fatigues, rucksacks on their backs, heading for the main gate. Their appearance means that the guard is back on duty at the back door of the dorm, and we only have a few minutes before the welfare officer heads back to Margie's room. We need to find Charlie.

I look around the parking area as we walk. There are maybe twenty vehicles here – Land Rovers, armoured cars, cargo vans – and people walking in all directions, shouting to each other, carrying crates and boxes and weaponry.

"Where is she?" Dan is looking nervous.

I'm trying to look as if I know where I'm going, but I'm looking around, trying to spot Charlie, and the vehicle she's grabbed the keys for. And then I see her, on the far side of the parking area, supervising the kitchen staff loading crates into the back of a camouflage pickup truck. We hurry over and join the back of her queue. She glances up and gives me a quick nod, then jumps up into the back of the truck. The man who has been stacking the crates looks confused, but she says something to him and he jumps down, walking back towards the kitchen. We hand our armour and belongings up to her, and she stacks them carefully next to the kitchen supplies before jumping down, closing the tailgate, and covering the back of the truck with a canvas sheet.

"Help me with this?" She asks, and I step over to tie the canvas down. "Is this her?" She asks, nodding towards Margie. I nod. "Good. Get her into the back seat." I signal to Dan, and he takes Margie to the far side of the truck, next to the fence, and helps her into the cab. I send Saunders to sit with her, and Dan helps him climb in before closing the door.

I glance around. No one has noticed what we're doing yet. Charlie directs another member of kitchen staff to a different vehicle with her crate, and hisses in my ear.

"We need to go."

I nod. Charlie runs round to the driver's door and climbs in. Dan climbs into the passenger seat, and I'm about to open the back door of the truck when I recognise a member of kitchen staff loading a crate into the vehicle next to ours, and she recognises me.

"Hey!" She shouts. "It's Charlie's puppy!" She puts down her crate and swaggers over to me, taking in my kitchen uniform and marching boots. "That's not your style, honey," She says, a nasty tone to her voice. She prods my shoulder, hard. "You chickening out, recruit? You trying to get out of fighting?"

She turns to her companions, and shouts.

"We've got a deserter!"

A couple of heads turn, but most people are concentrating on delivering their crates to the right places, and running back to fetch more. I'm fighting panic. We're so close to getting Margie out of here, and I don't want to screw up now. I open my mouth to tell her to mind her own business, but we are interrupted by the sound of a whistle. Three blasts, followed by someone shouting about the prisoner. Now people are starting to pay attention.

That's it. We have to leave. There's a loud blast of noise from behind me as Charlie starts up the engine.

I turn to open the door, but the girl from the kitchen grabs my arm. Before I can think about it, I swivel towards her and land my fist in her shoulder. She cries out, and I pull away. I open the door and drag myself up as Charlie puts her foot down hard, and the truck jumps forward. Margie grabs my arm, and holds tight until I can pull myself inside.

The truck is lurching and bouncing as Charlie drives across the grass towards the main gate. There are people running towards us – guards, recruits, kitchen staff – and people running away from the path of the truck. I manage to fasten my seatbelt, then lean out to try and close the door. I see the Commander running out of the nearest building, shouting. Ketty and Jackson follow him, wearing fatigues but carrying guns.

For the first time, I realise that someone could get killed in this confusion. I lunge for the door and pull it closed as Charlie pulls the truck onto the gravel roadway and turns us to face the gates. Through the windscreen, I watch as Jake unlocks the gates, and steps back to wave us through. Amy is standing with the guards, obviously acting as the distraction again, but as they see us driving towards them, and realise that Jake is letting us out, they grab Amy's arms and hold her between them. She screams my name as we speed past them, spitting gravel and dust from our tyres. Charlie sees the look on my face in her rearview mirror.

"Sorry, Bex. We don't have time to stop." And I know she's right. The gates are in front of us now. Jake has opened one, and the other is hanging loosely on its hinges. I glance behind us, over the crates, and see Commander Bracken shouting. Ketty and Jackson raise their guns, and I shout to everyone to get down. There's a rattling noise as bullets hit the tailgate, and then the back window explodes. We're showered with glass, ducking down in the back seat.

Charlie keeps going, smashes through the gate, and hurls the truck onto the road, tyres screaming. I risk a glance back, and I see Jake, holding his arms out to us. Amy, slumped between the guards, her hands cuffed in front of her. Commander Bracken takes Ketty's gun, and sprints out of the gates to where Jake is standing. He's watching us drive away as he puts his gun to Jake's head.

And we're round a corner, into the trees, and I don't see what happens next.

Escape

Charlie drives us for an hour, speeding down tiny country lanes, blasting the horn to force other traffic to get out of our way. We stay off the main roads, and lose ourselves in a maze of tracks and narrow, winding back roads. We're heading north, with detours to the east and west as we trace a route through villages and farms. Charlie slows down through the villages, hoping that no one will remember a sedately-driven camouflage truck if the base tries to track us down.

The sky clouds over, and it starts to rain. Charlie pulls off the road onto a forest track, and parks the truck out of sight among the trees.

"So where are we going?" She asks Margie.

None of us has spoken since we left the camp, except to shout warnings to Charlie as we see signposts or other vehicles on the road. We all start talking at once.

"That was incredible!"

"Is everyone OK?"

"Did you see …?"

Charlie cuts us off. "There'll be time for this later. We're not safe yet. Margie – where do we need to get to?"

Margie names a forest, somewhere in mid-Wales. "There's a track. If we drive down it, they'll see us, and they'll decide whether to let us in."

Charlie searches in the door pocket, and pulls out a road atlas. She hands it to Dan. "Figure out where we are, and where we're going. Congratulations – you're the navigator." She opens her door. "Ten minutes, and then we're back on the road." And she jumps down and walks away until I can't see her between the trees.

I want to hug Margie, to thank Dan, to apologise to Saunders, but to my surprise I burst into tears instead. Margie puts her arm round me.

"You did it, Bex. You got me out. Thank you." I'm nodding and sobbing and gripping her arm with my hands. It is a while before I can speak.

"But Jake and Amy …" is all I can say, and I'm sobbing again.

"Hey!" Dan shouts from the front seat. "Bex. Don't. They helped us, they got us out, but if we'd stopped, we'd all be back there, locked up with Margie." Or worse, I want to say, but I'm not sure that anyone else saw the Commander with Jake as we escaped. I keep quiet.

I take some deep breaths, and rub the tears from my cheeks. I reach over and put my hand on Saunders' arm. There are tears on his face, too, and he hasn't said anything since we drove away from Amy.

We all climb down from the truck. I fetch a branch from a fir tree and use it to brush the broken glass from the back seats and foot wells. Saunders leans against the cab, staring into the trees. Charlie comes back from the woods, and gives me a quick hug before reaching into the truck and bringing out a cloth and a bottle of water. She wets the cloth and gently cleans Margie's face, then hands her the cold, soaked cloth to hold against her injured eye.

"I'm Charlie. You must be Margie?" Margie nods. "Nice to meet you."

"Thank you. Thank you for getting me out."

"Thank these crazy kids for that," she says, waving her hand at us. "Without them, I'd still be packing crates and sending underage fighters off to help the army. I'd rather be here."

I can still see Jake, reaching out to us. "But Commander Bracken …"

"Stuff Commander Bracken. He was trafficking you lot into front-line combat. His recruiters kidnapped you, and you just kidnapped yourselves right back. And his enemy spy." She nods at Margie, and looks around. "We should go. Do you know where we are, navigator?" Dan nods. "Think you can get us to where we're going?"

"I think so."

"Then what are we waiting for?"

She opens the door and climbs back into the cab. We all climb in, and she starts the engine and turns the truck round, Dan giving directions from the end of the track.

*****

We drive for another hour or two, on country lanes and quiet roads. We're heading west, towards Margie's rebel friends. Dan and Charlie are concentrating on getting us there without being found. Margie holds my hand and watches the road ahead. Saunders leans back in his seat, eyes closed. I can't tell whether he's awake or asleep. I rest my head on the window and watch the countryside as we drive. Hedgerows and fields, farms and woodland. This is what I thought we were trying to protect, and here we are, driving through it, doubtless reported as dangerous criminals ourselves, now.

I'm trying to understand. Have we done the right thing? If the government is destroying its own cities, and blaming it on the rebels, who were we working for? And who are we running to now?

Who are the good guys, and who are the bad guys – or is it all just shades of grey? Are the rebels planting bombs and attacking the government? If so, why are we looking to them for shelter? Is the government faking all the attacks? If so, why? And why is there a rebellion at all?

What am I missing?

Terrorists

"You're up, kid," calls Charlie. "Where are we going?"

Margie leans forward in her seat. "You're looking for a sign to Makepeace Farm. It's along here somewhere. Pull onto the track, and let me out to open the gate. Head down the driveway, slowly. They'll be watching you."

After a few minutes, we find the sign. Charlie turns off the road, and stops to let Margie out.

"Stay where you are, Saunders. I'll climb over you. Mine needs to be the first face they see."

She climbs down, closes the door, and walks slowly towards the gate, her hands raised in front of her. She's looking straight ahead, and giving whoever is watching plenty of time to recognise her. She reaches the gate, unhooks it from the gatepost and pulls it open. Saunders shifts over into the middle seat. Charlie drives slowly through, and stops to wait. Margie closes the gate, and hands still up in front of her, walks back to the truck. She climbs in, and straps herself into Saunders' seat.

"Drive slowly." She says, quietly to Charlie. "If I shout, you stop." Charlie nods, and sets off along the track.

From the road, the track leads into dense conifer forest. Fifty meters or so past the first trees, the track bends to the right, and we are no longer visible from the road. Charlie keeps up the slow, careful pace as the track swings left again, and continues towards a building ahead of us.

"When you reach the farmyard, stop the engine, and put your hands up where they can see them. That goes for all of you. Hands empty and visible."

There's a slapping sound as the atlas drops from Dan's knee to the floor. His hands are above the level of the dashboard. I put mine against the window to my left. We crawl closer to the farm buildings.

We reach the concrete farmyard, and Charlie stops the truck and kills the engine. She slowly brings her hands up and holds them above the steering wheel.

There's no one in the farmyard, and we sit for a while, waiting. Then the door to the farmhouse opens, and a man walks out, holding an old-fashioned rifle.

"Don't move," whispers Margie. "Just wait."

There's another man with a rifle, walking round the corner of the barn. I glance behind us, and see a man and woman, also armed, walking out of the trees. They walk up to the truck, guns trained on us. The first man opens the driver's door and points the rifle at Charlie.

"Get out!"

She shows him her hands, and then carefully jumps down from her seat onto the concrete. She keeps her hands where he can see them. He reaches out and grabs her by the hair, pushing her to her knees.

"You're not Margie. Where's Margie?" He shouts, pushing the gun in her face. She tilts her head towards the back seat.

Margie taps, lightly, on the window, and shows her empty hands. The woman opens the door, and moves the gun aside when she sees Margie, and the state of her face. She grips the gun with one hand, and offers Margie the other hand to help her down. She looks hard at Margie's face, then pushes her away across the yard.

"You!" The woman shouts at Saunders. "Get down here. And keep your hands where I can see them."

Saunders unclips his seatbelt and shuffles over to the door. He jumps awkwardly down and stumbles as his bad ankle hits the ground. He catches himself with his hands, and I hear the woman shout to get his hands up. I can't see him, kneeling next to the truck, and I'm hoping he's OK when the door next to me opens, and I'm looking into the barrel of another shotgun.

"Down!" I reach for the edge of the door, and carefully lower myself to the ground. Before the man can force me to my knees, I kneel, and put my hands behind my head. He keeps the gun pointed at me, and I tell myself to stay calm. Keep my hands up. Don't say anything.

The last gunman pulls Dan from the front seat, and makes him kneel on the muddy concrete.

There's a moment of silence, and I hear Margie's voice.

"Let them go, Will. They're my friends."

Someone laughs.

"They broke me out of the camp, and they got me back here. They're not armed."

"You're guaranteeing that?"

"I am."

There's a pause. "OK."

The man next to me grips my elbow and hauls me to my feet.

"Keep your hands up."

He leads me across the farmyard, after Dan and Charlie. Saunders is limping badly again, and Margie and the woman with the gun are helping him towards the house.

They push us inside, into a spacious farmhouse kitchen. There's an Aga, and a large wooden table surrounded by mismatched wooden chairs.

"Sit down," Will calls, as he leans his gun next to the door and cleans his shoes on the mat. "Keep your hands on the table, mind." His soft Welsh accent is at odds with his gruff, direct manner. He's an older man, his face lined and tanned from working outside.

The woman comes in with Margie and Saunders, while the others melt back into the trees with their rifles. Margie pulls out a chair and helps Saunders to sit, then fetches another chair and a cushion so he can elevate his foot.

"Anyone want to tell me what's in that truck?" Will asks, standing at the head of the table and glaring down at us.

Charlie speaks first. "Supplies, mostly. Rations and water, which you're welcome to. We've also got armour, fitted to these guys;" she waves her hand to indicate the three of us, "weapons to go with the armour, and some personal belongings."

Will grunts. "You and you," he barks, pointing at me and Dan, "come out and help me unload."

We follow him out into the farmyard. He helps us untie the cover and drop the tailgate, then Dan climbs onto the back of the truck and hands the crates down to me, one by one. I stack them into piles of armour, and piles of rations while Will watches. There's a duffel bag that must be Charlie's, and a bundle of clothes – staff uniforms and fatigues – which I stuff into the top of Charlie's bag.

"Show me the weapons," he says, when the truck is empty, and Dan has climbed down.

I open the top crate in the pile. It's Dan's – the chest panel of the armour is on top, his name stamped across it. I lift the armour, and pull out the rifle, keeping it pointed at the ground, and hand it slowly to Will.

He takes it, and turns it over in his hands. He holds it up and sights along the barrel.

"Flashy," he says, with a disapproving tone. "Is it any good?" He looks down at it, doubtful.

"Sure," I say. "It hits targets. Blows holes in things." He makes an affirmative noise, and hands the rifle back to me.

"How many of those?"

"Three. And three suits of armour to go with them."

"We'll take those," he says, nodding.

"The armour is custom made," I protest. "It fits the three of us." He nods.

"And what about the supplies?"

I open the top crate to show him ration bars, dried meal sachets, chocolate bars. He peers in and nods again.

"Bring those to the kitchen. The rest, we'll stack in the barn."

Dan and I shift the crates. We stack the weapons and armour in the corner of the barn, and bring the kitchen crates and bags into the house. Will empties our rucksacks and inspects the contents, but returns everything to us. The woman from the farmyard unpacks the food and water, sorting it into piles.

"Keys," Will demands, and Charlie pulls them out of her pocket. "Anything I need to know?" He asks, and Charlie shakes her head. He grunts, and heads outside to move the truck.

"He's putting it out of sight under the trees," says the woman as she stacks boxes of ration bars on the worksurface. "We don't want them tracking you from the air."

Will drives the truck round the far side of the barn. We sit in silence as the sound of the engine fades.

Charlie is the first to speak up. "So, Margie. Where are we, and do we get introduced?" She tips her head in the direction of the crates.

"Jo, come and meet everyone." Jo adds another handful of meal packs to one of the piles and comes over to stand at the end of the table, hands on her hips. She's tall, and fit, with shoulder-length brown hair. Margie introduces us, and Jo nods.

"You're from the camp? Did you enlist?"

Dan and I start speaking, but Margie cuts in. "They were all conscripted. Dan and Bex are from my school – we've known each other for years. Saunders is a friend from the camp. Charlie was on the kitchen staff, but she helped to get us all out. No one here has much fondness for the government."

Jo purses her lips and nods. "OK. Welcome, then. Will's going to want to talk to you before he lets you past this room."

"Of course," replies Charlie, giving Jo a smile. Jo turns away as the door opens, and Will strides in. He stamps the mud from his boots, then pulls up a chair at the end of the table. He doesn't return the keys.

"We need to talk about you lot. Who you are, why you're here. What we're going to do about you."

Jo fills the kettle and lifts the cover on the Aga while Will pauses, considering what to say next.

"Margie, you should go out back. The Prof's there, and she'll want to talk to you." He waves her away, and she grins.

"Dr Richards is here?" Will nods. "I'll see you all later. Will – be nice to my friends." He gives her a grumpy half-smile, and she jumps up and heads for an internal door, giving Jo a quick hug on the way past.

Will demands our names and ranks. He asks about the kitchen scrubs we're wearing, and how we managed to steal a truck. He asks questions about the camp, about our training, about the personnel on site. He asks what we know about the government's plans, and what we know about the attack on Leominster. I tell him I saw it first-hand, and he quizzes me about exactly what I saw, and what I know. Jo brings tea, and we all sit, happy to be explaining our experiences to someone who will listen.

Charlie endures the most hostile interrogation. She's not a recruit, and she doesn't have the training or the equipment that we've brought with us. Will is very suspicious of her motives for helping us to escape.

"Listen. I have no love for the government. I took the job they offered because I needed it. I don't approve of kidnapping school children to make soldiers out of them. I don't approve of showing them off to the cameras. And I don't approve of whatever went on with this attack. I'm here by accident – Bex asked for my help, she needed to get out, and I saw a way to hurt the people in charge. But I'm pleased to be here, and I'm not going to go running back to the RTS. The sooner they stop – the sooner we all stop – destroying this country, the better."

The light is fading by the time Will is content that we're not planning to betray his location or attack him in his sleep. The two men who were guarding the farmhouse swap places with the next shift, and lean on the kitchen counter chatting with Jo while Will asks his final questions.

I'm tired and hungry when Will sends us with Jo to find a place to sleep. We pick up our bags and follow her down a corridor and out through a back door, Saunders leaning on me to take the weight off his ankle. The trees are growing very close to the back of the house, and the air is thick with the scent of pine. There's a carpet of soft, brown conifer needles underfoot. Jo leads us along a narrow path under the trees to a small concrete building with a metal door. As we approach, the door opens and another guard with a rifle lets us in.

I glance back at the house, and Jo catches my eye.

"Will and a couple of the guards have rooms in the farmhouse. They make it look lived-in, and keep the attention away from the rest of us. Everyone else? We sleep down here."

She smiles, and steps inside.

It's a small room with a concrete floor and walls. There are no windows, but a bank of screens shows CCTV footage from outside, along with views of the farmhouse, farmyard, track, and gate. There's a woman watching the screens, who looks up and greets us as we walk in. Jo responds, and leads us across the room to another metal door, which opens onto a metal staircase, heading down.

Saunders looks around the room. "What is this place?"

And I have a sudden flashback to a school trip when I was much younger. Concrete walls, metal doors, underground chambers. "It's a nuclear bunker, isn't it?"

Jo nods. "Some survivalist nutcase built it for his family in the sixties. Kept it off all the maps. Will's owned it for ages."

We follow her down four flights of clanking metal stairs.

Safety

The bunker isn't what I'm expecting. It's not leaking and dirty, like a derelict building, but it isn't high-tech and exciting, either. There are three levels at the bottom of the stairs from the gatehouse, divided into dormitories, offices, workshops, common rooms, and storage. There's another kitchen with several large tables, a meeting room with maps and diagrams on the walls, and even a laundry and shower rooms. It's clean, but everywhere I look there's bare concrete and exposed pipework. Everywhere is busy. There are people talking in the meeting room, people relaxing in the kitchen, people using the washing machines. There's a whole shift of people asleep, waiting to cover security overnight.

Jo takes us to a couple of small rooms at the end of the dormitory corridor. There's a four-bedded room for me and Charlie, and a four-bedded room for Dan and Saunders. We drop our bags on the beds, and she shows us what to do in an emergency. There are emergency torches charging in sockets along every corridor. The assembly point is the underground kitchen, and she makes sure that we know how to find everything we need.

"Dinner in half an hour, bunker kitchen," she calls, as she leaves us to settle in.

It feels great to change out of the muddy kitchen uniform, and peel off the base layers I've been wearing all day. I put on a clean set of fatigues and head to the shower room to wash my face and brush my hair. By the time I get back, everyone is in fresh clothes. Charlie is wearing jeans and a T-shirt, and I realise that this is the first time I have seen her wearing anything but the white kitchen scrubs and her fleece. She looks less formal and more relaxed. I start to realise that we've taken her away from her job and her colleagues, and that whatever happens now, she can't go back.

"Thank you, for getting us out this morning. And for driving us here. You didn't need to do that."

"You wouldn't have made it if I hadn't."

"That's true. But I'm sorry we've dragged you into this."

"Don't worry about me. I wasn't staying there – not after what you saw in town."

I think for a moment. There's a question I've been meaning to ask, but it feels intrusive after everything Charlie has done for us.

"Charlie," I begin, hesitantly. "Why were you working with those people? With Commander Bracken?"

She looks at me, as if she's deciding how to answer. She sits down on her bed, and it takes her a while to reply.

"I was in trouble, Bex," she says.

I sit on my bed, facing her.

"What do you mean? What kind of trouble?"

She puts her head back and stares at the ceiling.

"Police trouble."

"Oh."

She looks at me again. "I got caught, doing something they didn't like." I nod, encouraging her to go on. "There was a group of us. We didn't like where things were going with the country. With the government. So we took some direct action."

"Direct action?"

"Nothing serious. Nothing dangerous. We just defaced some of their billboards. Spray paint. Slogans. Stickers. That sort of thing."

"Oh. OK." That doesn't sound too bad.

"It should have been fine. We took precautions. We were clever about it. But …"

"But you got caught."

"I did. My friends didn't. So the police pinned it all on me."

She pauses. "I'm sorry," I say, not sure how to react.

She nods. "I could have turned them in, told the police who they were, but I didn't, so it went badly for me. I was looking at a prison sentence. And then it turned out that they had a job going at Camp Bishop. They couldn't find anyone to run the kitchen. No one wanted to work in their camps – residential job, no personal life, lousy pay. They couldn't find anyone with the right experience, until they arrested me."

I nod again.

"I'm a trained chef. I used to run the kitchen in a restaurant." She smiles, faintly, at the memory. "So they gave me a choice. Prison, or Camp Bishop."

"And you'd lose your restaurant job, either way."

She nods. "And any chance of getting a good job again, with prison on my record."

I think about what she's said. I knew I was in the camp against my will, but I didn't know Charlie was trapped, too. We were all prisoners at Camp Bishop. And what Charlie did – getting us out when she's already in trouble? There's no way she'll get away with this.

"But you helped us. You helped us when you knew it would get you into more trouble."

She leans forward, and puts a hand on my knee.

"It's a pleasure to help. To get some of you away from the camp and the front-line cameras. You don't need that. You need a country that works and you need to go back to school. You need a chance to do what you want with your lives."

"But you – if they catch you …"

"Let's not get caught." She winks at me, smiling. "You're better off out here than you were in there."

"Thank you, Charlie."

I hope she's right.

*****

We meet up with Margie at dinner, and she introduces us to the team. The people here are a mix of ages and professions. There are plenty of academics, some ex-military personnel, a couple of journalists, and some people who couldn't stand by and watch the government steal power. And of course, there's Dr Richards.

"How are you two?" She asks me and Dan, as we help ourselves to casserole and potatoes.

"We're OK," says Dan, looking at me.

"I'm pleased to be out of the camp," I tell her, pushing away flashbacks of training, of the attack in town, of driving away and leaving Jake and Amy at the gate. The gun to Jake's head.

"Margie tells me that you saw what they did?"

I nod. "I went into town, after Margie told me about the attack."

"And you're convinced it was a government attack?"

"I am. I saw the weapons they used, and I saw the cleanup crews. They weren't afraid of the City Killers – they were acting as if it was all a game. They knew there weren't any people left in town."

"Why did you ask her that?" Dan sounds indignant. "Of course it was the government. If it wasn't you, then who else could it have been?"

Dr Richards gives Dan a surprised glance. "You've changed your tune!" Dan nods, and shrugs. "We just need to be sure that there are no other groups working with their own agendas. But I'm satisfied that you saw what you say you saw. It is their usual pattern – just on a much bigger scale than they've worked at before."

"You mean they've done this before?"

"Plenty of times. Most of the attacks they blame on us – that's them, making people afraid."

Dan shakes his head. "Why would they do that? What's the point of killing their own citizens?"

And I realise. "Power," I hear myself say.

Dr Richards nods. "Exactly."

And I can see it so clearly.

"They want people to be afraid, so they'll sign over more power to the government. They want to take away the vote – not just for now, but forever. They want to give their friends the contracts to build defences and shiny new armour. They want to be able to rule completely – and they want people to allow them to."

"They want people to *ask* them to." Dan finishes my thoughts for me, and puts his fork back in his bowl. "They want us to want them in power. They want that to be the only way we feel safe."

Dr Richards is nodding as we speak. "And they're willing to commit whatever atrocities it takes to make us afraid."

"So what's the point of resisting? What can we do about it?"

"That's what we're trying to figure out here. We want to find ways to resist that will make a difference. We choose our targets carefully – government sabotage, mostly – and we do our best to avoid civilian casualties. But we're working behind the scenes as well, trying to influence people in power, people who might not be happy with the power grab."

"How can we help?"

"Dad – Will – wants to talk to you all tomorrow."

"Will's your Dad?" The question is out of my mouth before I can think about it.

She smiles. "Yes. Will's my Dad."

"So all this," Dan waves a hand at the room, "is yours?"

She laughs at that. "Definitely not. This is all very much Dad's project. Dad's act of resistance. And he's going to want to talk to you about what you can do, and what you can offer. In the meantime, try to be helpful around here. Give a hand to whoever's on catering duty. Collect up the dishes, clean the tables, keep an eye out for things that need doing. I know it doesn't seem like much, but we'll find a role for you soon enough. For now, getting involved will help you make friends and show people here that you're on our side. Oh – and stay inside the bunker. We don't want you wandering off and getting lost in the forest."

*****

We eat, and after the meal Dan and I help to clear the plates and load the dishwashers. It's good to see Dan back in fatigues, his sleeves rolled up past his elbows. It feels normal, in the middle of all this.

Dr Richards is talking to Charlie, trying to find out how the training camps are run, and Saunders is cleaning the tables, hopping between them and using chairs for support. I can't help expecting Commander Bracken to walk in with the evening briefing, but everything here seems much more informal. Eating our meal with the legendary terrorists felt more like sitting with a family than the camp ever did, and since we entered the bunker we haven't been yelled at or ordered around at all. It feels great to be welcomed into the group, but I find that I'm expecting this to end. I can't accept that all these people are happy to have us living with them.

There's no briefing after the meal. People sit around in groups, drinking coffee and beer, and talking. There are several card games running by the time we've filled the dishwashers, and we head back to sit with Charlie and Dr Richards.

"Thank you for helping," Dr Richards says as we sit down. "I've been hearing about life at Camp Bishop from Charlie, and you'll be happy to know that there's no curfew here." She smiles, and continues. "But you might want to think about getting some rest. Breakfast is at seven, and I know that Will's hoping to talk to you in the morning."

I'm about to protest, when I realise how tired I am. I've been running on adrenaline for days, and Dr Richards is giving me permission to stop. Suddenly it's all I can do to keep my eyes open. I say goodnight, and make my way back to my room, yawning and trying to remember where I'm going. I push my bag onto the floor, crawl under the covers, and fall asleep before anyone has time to follow me.

Interrogation

After breakfast, Will gathers the four of us in the meeting room. Dr Richards joins us, and we sit at one end of the meeting table.

Will wants to hear details about the camp, about our training, and about our patrol experiences, but most of all he wants to know about what I saw in town. I explain the City Killers and the clean-up crews, and I find myself in tears as I talk about the empty cars, the rubble of the buildings, the belongings abandoned on the road.

When I've finished, Will looks at Dr Richards.

"Bex," she says, hesitating, "the clean-up crews. They were people you knew?"

"Only the ones who came to take the weapons away. The ones who were checking everything before that – they were people I'd never seen before. They had armour like ours, but black instead of grey, and they were talking to their commanders on the radio."

She nods.

"And the whole camp was empty on the day of the attack? No one stayed behind?"

Charlie answers, and explains about the NBC drill. "We all had to leave. Even the guards at the gate."

Dr Richards sits back in her chair, and Will leans forward, elbows on the table.

"Tell me again about your training regime."

We explain the morning run, out in public where people would see us; the training in using our weapons and armour; the assault course; and the afternoon briefings in dealing with the public, and following orders.

"The whole idea was to look after yourself. They didn't want us working as a team, and they didn't want us helping each other. We were expected to get ourselves through the training, and through the public patrols. We weren't supposed to worry about other people. We were only there for the cameras."

And I can feel myself getting angry again. The Senior Recruits, training us and punishing us, and still treating us as front-line dolls. Ketty, locking me out in the rain for helping Saunders. Jackson, punching my ribs while his friend pinned my arms against the ground.

"We weren't real soldiers. We were the pretty mask over the face of the army. We're the brave volunteers who put our lives on hold to protect the public – except that we didn't volunteer. We were given half an hour to pack and leave school, and no one gave us a choice."

"How many of you felt like this, Bex?" Dr Richards asks, softly.

"Everyone!" Dan's voice is loud in the quiet room. He shrugs. "Probably not the Senior Recruits. I think they all volunteered. But the rest of us? There were people who didn't really get it, who thought this was like a holiday from school, and then we'd be going back. There were probably people who preferred the training to studying. But most of us? All that training for a few hours of public showing-off? We're a PR exercise, nothing more. And *our* lives are on hold to make *them* look good – the people with the City Killers."

"Yeah." Saunders starts quietly, but his voice gathers force as he speaks. "No one helped when we couldn't do the training. The Senior Recruits just left us, so we'd have to look after ourselves. I'm only here because Bex brought me back when I twisted my ankle, and Dan helped me get my stuff together to leave the camp. Me and Jake and Amy ..." He pauses, and collects himself. "Me and Jake and Amy – we only made it through the training because Bex helped us. She encouraged us, and she lost time on her own training to give us all an extra hand or talk us through the hard stuff." He looks at me. "And I know she got into trouble for it. I know the Senior Recruits hurt her for helping me." He looks down. "And just so we could wear our shiny armour in public and make people feel safe." He thumps the tabletop in frustration.

I reach across the table and take his hand. He looks up, and I look him in the eyes. Squeeze his hand, and let it drop. I don't know what to say. I think about sitting outside the gate in the rain. I think about the assault course, that first day. And I think about leaving Amy at the gate. Jake's face as we drove away.

"We've left our friends at the camp." I'm trying to keep the tremor out of my voice. "Jake and Amy helped us to escape. We planned to bring them with us, but the Commander saw what they did, and we couldn't stop for them. The last thing I saw …"

But I can't bring myself to say it. To my surprise, Charlie speaks up.

"The last thing we saw was the Commander holding a gun to Jake's head. We have no idea what happened to him after that." She shakes her head. "Bex is right. We couldn't stop."

Dan and Saunders both look up in surprise, and I realise that they didn't see what happened, they don't know what they saw. Dan looks shocked, and Saunders – Saunders looks heartbroken, the colour draining out of his face.

Charlie continues. "These are kids we're talking about. Child soldiers. They were kidnapped from their lives, and dropped into a physical training regime for a government they thought of as the good guys. They've jumped through all the hoops, they've worked hard, they've taken the blows because they've had no choice, and then they've been paraded in front of cameras as nothing more than stuffed suits of armour. It's insulting, and it's immoral, and this shouldn't be happening to them."

Will and Dr Richards exchange a look, and Dr Richards turns to Charlie.

"How many of these camps are there? Do you know?"

Charlie shakes her head.

"No idea. I'm just a kitchen supervisor. I know we weren't the only training camp in the country, but I don't know how many others there are." She shrugs. "We were RTS Unit 77B, if that helps."

Dr Richards gives Charlie a warm smile. "It might. Thank you."

I think we've finished, but Will clears his throat. He's been taking notes in an incongruously pink notebook, and he taps his pen on the page.

"Tell me again about the trip to Birmingham."

I start to talk about the concert and the patrols, but he stops me.

"No – start from the beginning. Before you left the camp. What did you do?"

I think for a moment, and I realise what he wants to know. I explain about the armour, the weapons, and the crates. I run down our preparations in the morning: packing our armour and guns, carrying our crates to the coach, loading them into the luggage space. He nods, and takes more notes. I talk through the journey, and the unloading at the other end. I give him the details I remember of the marquee, the security passes, the radios. He nods, encouraging me to continue, as he writes everything down.

Dan and Saunders add in details I've forgotten, and Saunders talks through the radio protocols for the patrols. And I tell him about the cameras: TV cameras and photographers everywhere, documenting our presence, publicising our protection. The Press pass round the photographer's neck. The photos that he wanted for his newspaper. Front-line Barbie and her bestie. Jackson mocking us as we walked into the marquee.

"We were a joke to them," I whisper, through tears. "All this for a joke."

Dr Richards reaches over and takes my hand.

"Thank you, Bex. I think this could really help us."

*****

They talk to Margie next, and confirm aspects of our accounts. Over the next few days, Will stops me in the corridor, or at meals, to ask more questions.

"He's planning something," I tell Dan one night, as we're walking back to our rooms. "He's asking me for all the details, and they add up to something big."

"Anything we can do to strike back." Dan has seen what the government can do, and he's as angry with them now as he was with Margie at school for opposing them. He must feel betrayed by the people he trusted to look after us.

"You'll help?"

"Instantly. I'm sick of the government getting away with this. And I'm sick of being the sticking plaster on their public image." He stops, and turns to me. "And I really want to get Jake and Amy out of there. I can't believe we left them behind. What the Commander did …"

"We had to! We couldn't stop!"

"I know. But we shouldn't have left them."

I nod. "We let them down. I know that. If there's anything we can do …"

"We'll do it."

"Yeah. We will."

AUGUST

Demonstration

Our chance comes sooner than I expected.

Our days have settled into a new rhythm. Breakfast at seven. Briefing from one of the rebels – usually Will, but sometimes it's Dr Richards, or one of the other leaders of the group. Help with the clearing up, help with general housework. I've convinced Jo to take me and Dan for a run every day – through the forest, as far as the lake that feeds our water supply, and back. It means that we get some fresh air and exercise, but someone keeps an eye on us and checks that we don't wander off, or send messages to government troops.

We come back and shower, then help make lunch. Afternoons are mostly free for cards and talking, and some basic lessons on the politics of the conflict from Dr Richards. I find myself enjoying this return to studying, and I think Dr Richards appreciates having an audience to teach again.

A week after our meeting with Will, he stops me in the corridor after breakfast.

"Think you can teach some of us to use that armour of yours? And the guns?"

I think about it. The armour is made to fit us, but I'm sure it would fit some of the younger people here. Training other people can only help us to strike back, and to help Jake and Amy. I nod. "Sure."

"Find me in the meeting room after lunch. Bring Dan and Margie."

"And Saunders?"

"Not with his injured ankle. I'll find something else for him do."

I find Dan in his room, getting ready for our run with Jo.

"Are you up for training people how to use the suits and guns?"

"If it helps, of course. When?"

"After lunch. We need Margie, too."

"I'll put it on my incredibly busy schedule," he says, and grins.

*****

We assemble in the meeting room after lunch: me, Dan, Margie, and Will. Someone has brought the crates down from the barn, and left them on the table.

"Start by unpacking your boxes, and telling me what's in there."

I reach into the kitchen crate where I hid my armour. It's obvious that someone else has already been through the contents of the crate, and packed it again – nothing fits properly, and my careful way of nesting the pieces of the armour together to save space has been messed up and ignored. I pull out my helmet, and all the plastic panels that make up the suit. I check the radio and the contamination panel, and make sure that nothing has been lost or damaged. Dan does the same, and we stack the armour carefully on the table.

"Where's the gun?" Dan sounds upset, and gives Will a defiant look.

Will stays calm. "Armour first. We'll move on to weapons later. Is this everything?"

"We have base layers that we wear underneath, and the boots we're wearing. Other than the guns, yes. That's the armour."

"Can you show me how it works?"

I peel off my T-shirt and uniform trousers. I'm wearing the base layers underneath. I've learned to apply my own armour, so I go about attaching the panels to the base layers, and explaining what I'm doing at every point.

Will and Margie listen, and pay attention to the details – how the armour fits together, which pieces attach to each other, how the air canister connects with the other panels, how the radio controls work.

Lastly, I pick up the helmet and twist it into place. Immediately, the sound from the room is muted, and I can hear my own breathing. It is strange to be wearing this in the bunker, and for the first time I notice all the background noises that disappear when the helmet clicks into place. There are air conditioning units, ventilation fans, conversations from neighbouring rooms – all gone. I'm in a world of my own, protected and distant from everyone who wants to use me for their own schemes.

It's a good feeling.

Will is signalling to me to remove the helmet. Reluctantly I twist it, disconnect it from my armour, and place it on the table in front of me. The sounds of the bunker return, and once again I'm in someone else's space, imprisoned and forbidden from leaving. My breathing gets faster and I'm close to panic. I realise Dan is talking and I focus on his voice.

"You're OK. You're OK, Bex. Come on – sit down." He takes my hand and guides me to a chair, crouches beside me. "You're safe. We're safe."

I grip his hand, and feel my heart rate slowing.

"OK?"

I take a deep breath and nod.

"OK."

Will has been watching my reaction, and Dan's. Margie looks at Will, a concerned look on her face.

"She's been through a lot, Will," she says. "Give her time."

Will grunts, and picks up the back panel of Dan's armour.

"What are the clips for?"

"That's for the gun," Dan explains, miming the action of clicking the gun into place over his shoulder. He gets it right, even with no gun in his hand. I smile, recognising the hours of work that went into learning that action.

Will puts down the armour. "Right. Let's bring the others in."

Margie goes to the door, opens it and calls down the corridor. I hear footsteps, then four young men and two young women hurry into the room.

Will uses me as the model, and asks Dan to talk through the pieces of the armour, demonstrating how they work together. The young rebels watch and listen, reaching out to touch an arm plate, the gun clips, the radio controls on my glove. They handle the pieces that Dan is explaining, and watch closely as we show them how everything fits together.

It is a relief to be able to stand still and not have to find the words to explain the suits. I let Dan do the talking, and turn to show off different parts of the armour as he describes them. Now I really am Front-line Barbie. The thought makes me laugh.

*****

Will dismisses the rebels and asks us to return after lunch tomorrow. He wants us to train them to put on, wear, and use the armour, and eventually the guns as well. I strip off the armour pieces and stack them neatly in my kitchen crate, then pull my trousers and T-shirt back on over my base layers.

Will dismisses us, too. "Get changed, and take your base layers to Jo in the workshop."

I give him a confused look.

"She's going to make more of them," Margie says, laughing at the look on my face. "We need base layers for everyone if we're going to train them properly. Don't worry – you'll get them back!"

Dan and I leave our crates on the table and head back to our rooms. I change out of my base layers, and meet Dan in the corridor. He's dug out his and Saunders' leggings, tops, and gloves, and we carry our bundles of black fabric down the corridor to the workshop.

Jo is waiting, with a sewing machine and a notepad of measurements from the rebels we'll be training. She thanks us, and takes the clothes, checking them for labels and rubbing the fabric between her fingers.

"I think I can replicate these. Thank you for letting me have them. I'll get them back to you as soon as I can."

And I walk away, wondering why she thinks I had a choice.

Weapons

Armour training takes a couple of weeks. At first, there's only one set of base layers, so our trainees have to take it in turns to put the armour on and get used to wearing it, but over the course of a few days, Jo makes up six more sets of base layers, and returns ours to us. With three sets of armour, and everyone ready to put it on, we can race one trainee against another; demonstrate a movement technique using one of us and one of them; and start to teach them how the radios and contamination panels work.

It is surprisingly enjoyable, teaching our skills to people who want to learn. I start to realise how much we learned at the camp, and how my skills have developed since our first day wearing the armour. The rebels are quick to learn, and enthusiastic. I find myself concentrating on the task of making them all competent, and I start to forget what we're doing this for.

And then one afternoon Will welcomes us to a training session, and puts three guns on the table. I'm happy to see our weapons again, and that we are being trusted to handle them, but I realise that we have a long way to go, teaching the rebels how to use them.

We begin by teaching them how to clip the guns into the armour. It takes hours to get used to this action, lining the gun up and sliding it into the clips behind you and out of sight, and for the first time I am frustrated with the rebels. They're all so clumsy, and the process is so slow. It is such a simple movement, when you figure it out, but it takes a long time to get there.

It takes days, but eventually they can all stow their guns – not all of them on the first attempt, but it's good enough. Now we need to teach them to shoot.

I stay behind after a training session to talk to Will. He's happy with their progress, and, like me, he wants to move on to using the guns.

"Are they ready?" I nod. "Tomorrow, then." And he leaves the room.

*****

The next day, Will takes us out of the bunker. We pass the guard in the entrance hall, and Saunders is there, watching the screens with one of the rebels. He gives us a cheerful wave.

"They've found you a job, then?" Dan sounds impressed, and gives Saunders a high five on the way past. "You've kept that quiet!" Saunders grins, and spins side to side on his office chair.

"Indoors and sitting down!" He drags his chair back towards the screens. I notice that he's still only using one foot – the injured ankle he holds above the floor.

I can't help grinning back. "Take good care of us, Saunders. You're our front line of defence now!"

He nods, and tries to look serious, but he can't hide his proud smile. I notice his sketch of all of us in our armour, propped up on the table under the screens.

The guard lets us out, and Will leads us up to the farmhouse, and round the side of the building to the barn. Dan and I carry the crates of armour and guns, and the rebels are all wearing their base layers under sweat pants and T-shirts. We select two to put on the armour, and time them getting ready. They're not bad. There's room for improvement, but they're getting better.

Will lines up a target at the far end of the barn, propped up on bales of straw. Dan demonstrates clipping in a magazine, taking the safety off, lining up the target, and firing. His bullet tears through the target, and the straw, and leaves a ragged hole in the wall of the barn. Will looks impressed.

We rebuild the target with planks of wood and more bales of straw, and the trainees have their chance to try the guns. There's a lot of work to do, but they've all got the basic idea. We need to work on their confidence with the weapon, and with their aim – but that's just a matter of practice. I can see that, given enough time, we will be able to train them to hit the target quickly and cleanly almost every time.

But after the session, Will sits us down in the farmhouse kitchen, while the trainees go back to the bunker.

"You've got three days. Can you train them?"

"Three days? Why?" I'm breathless. What does he mean?

"We move in four."

"Move where?" Dan sounds as surprised as I am.

"We've had intelligence. There's a target we can hit. Three days. Can you do it?"

I look at Dan, and he shakes his head.

"No. No, we can't. They need time to get used to the guns." Will glares at Dan.

"Wait," I say, fighting rising anger. "Why do they have to use the guns? Why can't we?"

Will shakes his head. "We're going after your RTS friends. You think you can hold guns to their heads?"

I hesitate, but Dan answers quickly, "Yes. Yes, I do. Because most of them aren't our friends." He looks directly at Will, challenging him to disagree.

I think about holding a gun to Ketty's head. Or Jackson's. Or Commander Bracken's.

"Yes. I think we can."

Will shakes his head. "We only get one shot at this. One chance to get what we need."

"And what's that?"

So Will explains his plan.

Decision

Training is intensive for three days. We work with the rebels morning and afternoon, giving them plenty of experience with hitting targets and handling the weapons. By the third day, all of them can unclip the gun, hit the target, and re-clip it most of the time. We have to be careful not to waste our bullets – we don't have many to spare. For dedicated target practice, we switch to Will's old-fashioned shotguns.

On the third day, Will asks Dan and me to demonstrate our skills with the guns, and we prove that we can unclip, hit the target, and re-clip under pressure. He looks satisfied, and confirms that we'll move out for our ambush in the morning.

We have one task to complete before we wear this armour outside again. Will understands, and hunts through a box in the back of the barn until he finds what we need. Dan and I spend the hour before dinner with our armour pieces propped against the straw bales, spray painting every panel black, and erasing our names from the torso sections. When we're done, the armour looks like the suits I saw in town, the clean-up crews working on the City Killers. There were no names on their armour – just anonymous black panels.

"We've done it. We've disrespected our armour. We've disobeyed Batman's number one rule!" Dan laughs, and kicks an empty paint canister across the barn floor.

It might not be the first time we've stood up to Commander Bracken, but Dan's right – this does feel important. As if we've admitted our treason, accepted our disobedience. It feels like the point from which we can't go back.

We spend the evening with Saunders, Charlie, Margie, and Dr Richards. After dinner, we gather at a table in the kitchen and talk about the plans for tomorrow. We know what we're expected to do, and that our trainees will be helping us. I'm worried, but I think Will's plan will probably work. We just can't guarantee what the government response will be, or be completely sure that our intelligence is accurate.

I head off early to get some sleep, and Charlie comes back to our room just as I'm getting into bed. She sits down on her bunk, opposite mine, and leans her elbows on her knees, shoulders hunched over, hands clasped together.

"Are you sure you want to do this?"

I sit down, too, our knees almost touching in the narrow room.

"I'm sure. I think we have a good chance to hit them where it hurts, and get ourselves an advantage. I'm pretty happy with the guys we've been training. So … yeah. Why not?"

She looks at me and shakes her head. "That's not what I meant."

I take a deep breath. "I know."

"Are you sure you want to be someone else's frontline doll?"

"It's not like that," I begin, but I know it is. Charlie looks at me, coldly.

My shoulders slump. "OK. It is like that. But I think we can help. I think we can do this."

"You're letting yourself be used again. You're a kid, not a soldier –"

"I'm a kid *and* a soldier." I talk over her, forcing her to listen – because she's wrong about this. "I was a kid when all this started, but I've seen things, and I've learnt things, and I've messed up. I can fight, and I can win. I can see what the government is doing, and I can understand that I *want* to fight back."

"So you're doing this for yourself?" Charlie's voice hasn't softened. She's angry with me, and she's angry with Will.

"Yes? No." I shake my head. "I don't know. All I know is that I have the skills and the experience to help the rebels, and that's what I want to do tomorrow. If I get to hurt the government, then even better. But this is what I want to do."

She bows her head, runs her hands through her hair, looks up at me.

"OK. If you're sure you know what you're doing." She puts her hand on my knee. "Be careful, Bex. Don't let them use you. Don't let them see you as disposable. Make sure you come back."

It's as if she's hit me. I haven't thought about not coming back. Will has approved of our shooting skills and our training of the other rebels. We've got a target and a plan. I know what to do. I haven't considered what could happen if something goes wrong. I've got my armour, my gun, and my training, and backup from Will and the others. I'll be fine.

But I can't find anything to say to reassure her. I clasp her hand, and nod in agreement. She reaches over and puts her arms round my shoulders.

"Be safe, Bex," she whispers. She gives my shoulders a squeeze, then stands up and leaves the room, closing the door on her way out.

Raid

I'm lying, in my armour, in a ditch at the side of a narrow road. Dan is beside me, and so are two of the rebels we've been training. The other four are in the ditch opposite. Will is in one of the trucks, out of sight in the trees behind us. We're waiting for his signal.

We left the bunker early this morning, driving two pickup trucks, with two crates of armour in the back. We drove for an hour or so, then Will turned off the road into the woods, and the other truck followed. Dan and I changed into our armour while Will handed out guns and bullets to our trainees. He ran through the plan again, and sent us to get into position for the raid.

It's been raining, and there's water in the ditch, threatening to flow over the tops of my boots. We're leaning against the side of the ditch, our heads level with the road surface. The trees overhang the road here, so my view is blocked by a curtain of dripping leaves. Once again, I'm outside in the cold and wet in my armour. This time, I'm waiting for Will's order to move.

Dan and I have checked our radios, and tuned the channel to Will's radio in the truck. With my helmet on I can hear my own breathing, and the faint gurgling of the water in the bottom of the ditch. And then, something else. I can hear the noise of an engine approaching. My heart begins to beat faster, and my muscles tense, waiting for Will's signal. Dan tenses beside me, ready to run.

"Go!" Shouts Will, the radio speaker loud in my ear, and we pull ourselves out of the ditch, duck under the branches and run to the middle of the road, guns sliding smoothly from their clips and pointed ahead, at the approaching vehicle.

It's a coach, like the one we used to travel to Birmingham. Coming round the corner in the road towards us, travelling quickly. We hold our ground as the driver sees us in the road, and registers the guns. He slams on the brakes, and the coach starts to skid on the wet surface.

My heart is hammering in my chest as I try to stand still and calm in the path of the sliding vehicle. The back end starts to swing, and I'm watching in slow motion as the front of the coach starts to angle away, and the side turns towards us. We both take a step back as the coach slows and stops, brakes screaming, rear end hanging over the ditch. There's a moment of stillness, and I see a line of shocked faces staring out of the windows at us.

Recruits, in uniform. I make myself look away. I don't want to see people I recognise.

The engine cuts out, the coach shivering as it stops. In the sudden silence, Dan and I walk towards the luggage compartment. I aim at the locks on the compartment hatches, and each one pops open as the bullets hit. We drag the hatches all the way up, and start to unload the crates inside on to the roadway.

Two more rebels jump out from the ditch behind us and take over, with two more acting as a human chain to get the crates as far away from the coach as possible on the road. Dan and I head round to the front of the coach, keeping our guns trained on the driver and the front-seat passengers. Dan stands in the road, gun aimed at the windscreen, while I step carefully round to the door. Two more of my trainees are already in position, rifles pointed into the coach.

I have to remind myself that no one knows who I am. My name is no longer painted across the front of my chest, my helmet is on and my visor is down.

"Talk to me!" Will's voice on the radio.

"We're securing the coach now. The crates are being unloaded." Dan sounds confident.

"Just checking for anyone who wants to pick a fight. Oh – and Will? The coach is blocking the road. You'll need to approach from the North."

"Good work." And he's gone.

All we have to do is hold the coach here while the crates are unloaded, and transferred to the trucks. We need everyone to stay on board, and we don't need anyone trying to be a hero. I keep my gun pointed at the door, and gesture to the trainees to go and help with the crates.

I think we're going to make it. I can hear the sound of an engine growing louder, and I'm hoping that's Will and the other truck. The quicker the crates can be loaded the better, and then we can drive away and disappear.

"Approaching now." I can hear the two trucks as they swing round in the road, and the trainees shouting to each other as they load up the crates.

I glance up at the windows, and I notice that the line of faces is gone. Someone is giving orders inside the coach, and the recruits have all ducked their heads down, or moved away from the windows, out of the line of fire.

I take a breath to report this to Will, just as I hear a gunshot, and the sound of breaking glass. Dan makes a strange grunt over the radio and goes quiet. I want to move – I want to check on Dan, but I need to guard the door. My thoughts are racing, and as I'm deciding what to do next, the second door of the coach opens, halfway down the side where I'm standing. Someone leans round the edge of the doorway and points a handgun at me, and I freeze.

I'm wearing armour. I can probably take a hit, but if I'm unlucky they'll catch the base layer and the bullet will go right in. I'm splitting my attention between the front door and the gun, making an effort to take deep, steady breaths and clear my mind. The holder of the gun is keeping their head inside the coach for now, and the front door is closed. If I can avoid escalating the situation, we can still get away.

I swing my gun so it is aimed at the second door, and take a step back, towards the front of the bus. I'm breathing steadily, willing everyone to stay calm. There's no need to fire. We're not trying to hurt you. We just want the armour.

There's a shout over the radio, and I jump in surprise. I try to focus on the coach in front of me, and the hand holding the gun. The driver, sitting with his hands held up in front of him.

"What's going on? Bex?"

I try to speak, but I'm out of breath. I'm worried about Dan. I'm terrified that the person with the gun is going to do something stupid. I'm in control of the situation, and it's up to me to keep everyone safe. I almost laugh – this is exactly what the camp was training us for. Don't rely on your team – rely on yourself. Get yourself out of danger. Get yourself on camera. Get yourself seen.

And I know what I have to do. They have to see me, and they have to see that we're serious.

"I'm handling it," I say to the radio. "Just be ready to go. Dan?"

"Bex. I'm OK. They've got a gun on me, and they've dented my armour, but I'm OK."

"Will! Get some guns pointed at the coach! I need to give them a reason to stop shooting."

"Done." I can hear Will shouting at the trainees, distant, outside my helmet.

I take two deep breaths, then step forward and fire bullet after bullet into the second doorway. The hand with the gun fires twice, wildly, missing me entirely and landing bullets in the trees next to the road. The shooter pulls the gun back, shelters in the stairwell of the coach, so I step closer, firing into the opening. There's some shouting from inside, and the door closes.

I step away and point my gun at the front door again.

No one moves. There's no sound from the radio. I step forward and bang my fist on the door, pointing to the driver's console. The driver looks at me, and lifts his hands above his head. I point again, and, keeping his eyes on me, he reaches forward to unlock the door.

The front door opens with a faint sigh. I push myself against the door frame, and aim my gun up into the aisle. There's someone standing in line with the front seats, face in shadow, holding a gun like mine. Pointing it at Dan through the star-cracked front window. I risk a glance out of the front of the coach. Dan is standing on the road, hands in the air, gun above his head. There are two trucks pulled up behind him, loaded with crates, canvas tied down on top. And there are six trainees armed with Will's rifles, all pointed this way.

I try to talk to the people on the bus, but I realise that they can't hear me through the helmet. There's no loud-speaker in this armour – I'm only a front-line doll, after all – I'm not supposed to do any real fighting. I use one hand to crack open the visor, just enough for my voice to be heard.

"Drop the gun!" The person looks at me in surprise, and I realise it's Ketty. Will was right about our target.

"Drop the gun!" I shout, much louder. She smirks, so I take aim at her chest and she quickly lets go of the rifle. It clatters to the floor next to her feet.

"Kick it to me." She kicks it down the steps, past the driver, a sour look on her face.

I take another step up into the coach.

"Sit down." I wave the gun at her again, and she steps back and lowers herself into a seat. I climb up next to the driver, until I can see all the way down the aisle.

The recruits are crouching, in the aisle and next to the seats, hands over their heads. One or two glance up at me, and I realise that I recognise their faces.

"What are you doing?" Will's voice over the radio.

"Not now." I keep my voice quiet – the radio will pick up a whisper if it needs to.

"Get out here."

"Not yet. There's something I need to do. Dan – can you cover the back door?"

"On my way."

I haven't heard the second door opening again, but I need someone standing guard.

"Heads up! Back in your seats!" I shout, as loudly as I can. The recruits look at each other, but they don't move. I wait a moment, and then raise the gun to the ceiling and fire one shot.

"Do as they say!" Someone shouts from half way down the coach, and I know it's Jackson. He must be the shooter at the back door.

The recruits scramble to their feet and back into their seats. I'm watching them carefully, and I see Jake, keeping his head down and sliding into a seat close to the front. I take another step up, next to Ketty, and I point my gun at Jake.

"You! On the ground." He looks confused, then stands up out of his seat and lies down in the aisle. His face is white, and he's shaking. I look around, but I can't see any more faces. Everyone is hidden by the seats in front of them. I need to find Amy.

I know this wasn't part of the plan. I know we can drive away now if we want to. We have what we came for, and the trucks are ready to go. But this might be my last chance to rescue Jake and Amy. I need to find her, but I can't afford to move any further into the coach.

"Stand up!" I wave the gun, and the recruits slowly get to their feet, holding themselves up against the headrests. I look around, and I have another idea. I need to make this look like a hostage-taking.

"You! And you!" I pick two recruits at random. "On the floor". I'm running out of time. They step into the aisle and lie down. I still can't see Amy.

"Back row! All of you, in the aisle, now!" And there she is.

"You! On the floor. The rest of you – back to your seats."

Four recruits on the floor. Jackson on the stairs to the second door. Dan outside, covering his escape.

"Here's what's going to happen," I call out, explaining myself to Will as much as to the people on the bus. "These four soldiers are going to leave the bus with me. They're coming in the trucks, and we'll drop them off a mile down the road. You can come and fetch them. But you fire on us; you try to stop us; you do anything stupid; and we take them with us. Understood?"

There's a grunt from Ketty, next to my elbow, and silence from the back of the coach.

"Am I understood?"

"Understood, terrorist," shouts Jackson, and Ketty swears.

And then too many things happen at once.

Ketty reaches over and pushes my elbow, hard. I lose my balance, and fall into the seat across the aisle. It's an empty seat – Jackson's? – and I struggle to get back on my feet. The second door of the coach hisses open, and someone fires two shots. I can hear the sounds of a struggle, then another shot. Someone runs up the steps, shouting, but I'm too busy pulling myself up to see who it is. Ketty is on her feet, turning towards me with her fists raised, aiming for the faceplate of my helmet. I'm trying to stand up and keep hold of my gun, and the first blow knocks my head back painfully. I brace for more. The radio is loud with shouting. There are voices coming from inside the bus, and I can't understand what anyone is saying. I wait for the next punch to land, but instead there's another gunshot and Ketty's fists fall away. I drag myself up, my knee on the seat, and turn towards the back of the coach.

"Dan!"

He's standing in the aisle, kicking the recruits I picked out and yelling at them to stand up. They do, and he grabs the shirt of the closest, and hurls him down the back steps.

"Get out! Get down the steps!" He's screaming at them, and they're cowering, trying to move past him and out of the coach. I risk a glance out of the windows, and see two of the trainees, rifles up, outside the second door, directing the recruits to the front of the coach and out to the trucks. I step into the aisle, turning towards the front steps, gun in one hand, and find myself looking down the barrel of Ketty's gun.

She's lying on her back next to the driver, a patch of red growing on the camouflage fabric around her knee. She's biting her lip, and her leg is braced against the bottom step, but she's picked up her gun and it's pointing at my head.

I have no idea what is going on behind me – where Jackson is, where Dan is – all I can see is the dark, rifled barrel, and Ketty's hands, shaking, her finger on the trigger.

Slowly, I raise my hands, clasping the barrel of my gun in one hand and opening the other to her, palm first. There are tears in her eyes, and I think she's trying not to cry out. I brace for a shot that I'm not sure my helmet can handle.

There's the sound of smashing glass, and Ketty drops her gun, shielding her face with her arms. I look up, and realise that the windscreen has shattered, showering Ketty with sharp fragments. Someone grabs the back panel of my armour and drags me back down the coach, down the steps, and onto the road. Jackson is lying at the bottom of the steps, clutching at his chest. I can't tell whether he's breathing.

Dan spins me round and lifts my visor.

"Trucks. Now!" He shouts, and grabs my elbow, dragging me to the front of the coach and over to where Will and the others are waiting.

The recruits I've picked out are already in the back seat of one of the trucks, crammed into a space for three. While our trainees divide themselves between the remaining seats, Will points us to the back of the pickups.

"You're on guard duty!"

We climb up onto the backs of the trucks and sit on top of the canvas, guns pointing back at the coach. Will checks that everyone's in, then climbs into the driving seat of one of the trucks and they both pull away, gently, along the road. Through my raised visor I watch as we drive away. The driver, sitting with his hands in the air. The back of the coach hanging over the ditch. No sign of Ketty or Jackson.

The trucks turn a corner in the narrow road, and the coach is hidden behind the trees. I drop my gun onto my lap and wrench my helmet from my head, fighting for breath. I'm trying to pick apart what happened, to understand what we've just done. I close my eyes and hold tight as the truck swings round corners and the crates shift under me.

When we stop, a mile down the road, I'm shaking. I let go of my gun and my helmet, and drop myself down over the side of the pickup. Will climbs down, opens the back door, and shouts at the recruits to get out. Two of them climb down, looking stunned, but I wave to Jake and Amy to stay put.

"They're coming with us," I whisper to Will. He looks at me, clearly unhappy with the way things happened on the bus, but backs down when he sees my determination. He turns to the others.

"Go back to the bus. Stay here. Whatever you want. You're safe now."

They look around at us, confused, recognising me and Dan and trying to put the pieces together.

"Go on," I shout at them. "Go!" And they set off back along the road, glancing nervously at us and our guns.

I pick up my helmet and gun, and climb into the back seat with Jake and Amy. Dan climbs into the other truck, and we set off again, keeping to quiet roads, taking off-road detours along forest tracks, and turning back onto country lanes.

I lean back, as much as I can in my armour, and rest my head against the top of the seat.

"I assume you want to come with us?" I ask, not looking at Jake and Amy. I'm staring at the ceiling, too exhausted to lift my head and talk to them directly. "Jake?"

"What are you doing here, Bex?" Amy sounds as drained as I am, the adrenaline wearing off.

"Coming back for you." I manage to turn my head towards them. "And I'm very relieved to see you both alive. We weren't sure, after …"

Jake cuts in. "You left us there, Bex! You drove away and you left us. Commander Bracken held –"

"I know. I saw."

"You saw the gun and you *drove away*?"

"There wasn't anything they could have done." I sit up, surprised to hear Will defending me.

"You could have come back. Later. Broken us out."

I spread my hands in a frustrated gesture, indicating me, them, the truck.

"Thanks, Bex," whispers Amy. "I knew you wouldn't leave us there."

Jake stares stubbornly out of the window, too angry with me to speak.

Reckoning

Will is furious. I'm sitting at the table in the meeting room with Dan and the trainees, and Will is standing at the end of the table, shouting. We've made it back to the base, and we've unloaded the crates – into the bunker, this time. Jake and Amy have been assigned bunks in our rooms, and they're off somewhere with Jo and a delighted Saunders, settling in.

And this is where I answer for my actions.

I've tried to explain the training, the expectation that while I'm wearing that uniform, I solve my own problems. Dan has backed me up, and been shouted at as well. I'm not going to apologise for rescuing Jake and Amy, so I sit and listen while Will tells me all the things I did wrong.

"You put all of us in danger. All of us. You took the fight onto the coach. You escalated the situation, and you gave the government even more reasons to come after us. You showed them, clearly, that you're one of them, working for us. You engaged directly with our targets, and you humiliated people who you know will not take that lightly. And, worse – the government thinks we're holding two hostages, thanks to you.

"What were you thinking? What insanity forced you to do those things? You shot two Senior Recruits …"

Dan speaks up. "Actually, I did …"

"I'm not interested! Why do you think that's any better?" Will's face is red with anger, and he's pacing up and down across the table from us. I've never seen him angry before, and I don't know how this will end. I try to stay calm. I know I did the right thing, and I know I used a language the government will understand. Be public, be seen, and show them what you can do.

Will throws his hands in the air in frustration, and sits down at the head of the table. He beckons to someone behind me, and I realise that Dr Richards has slipped into the room during the shouting. She steps up to the table, and stands between us and Will.

"Dan. Bex. It's good to have you back. I'm glad no one got hurt." She pulls out a chair and sits down. Her voice is measured and calm, and it's a shock to be treated so gently after Will's outburst.

"I understand why you did what you did, and I gather that the two of you make a formidable team on the front line. So thank you. We have the armour, and we have the guns. We even found two crates of ammunition, so we're well supplied for now.

"Will's concern," she glances at Will, who nods, "is that this will provoke the government into some extreme actions against us. They are likely to stage more terrorist attacks, and blame them on us. They'll use the public outrage to prioritise finding us and shutting us down. We're are in very real danger now, and the bloodshed has hardly started.

"So the plan is to hit them first, and hit them hard. With the armour and the guns, we have some limited ability to infiltrate government buildings and events. We need to use that ability fast, before they tighten their security.

"You'll be training more of us to use the guns and the armour. All of you." She indicates our existing trainees around the table. "We need as many people as possible trained in armed response, and you're our best tutors."

Dan and I nod, surprised that we're not being dismissed for our actions.

Will puts his hands on the table and leans towards us. "If you two ever put us in danger again," he looks us both in the eyes, deliberate and angry. "Ever – I will leave you behind. I will leave you to be picked up by *them*, and you can take your chances with the people you deserted, stole from, and shot.

"Is that clear?"

I nod, and clasp my hands together to stop them from shaking.

"Clear."

"Good."

Consequences

The training continues. We start the next day, with ten new trainees. We show them how to put on the armour, how to handle the guns, and we take them to the barn for target practice with Will's rifles. We have to find suits that fit the trainees, but thanks to the raid on the bus, we have plenty to choose from. We took plenty of ammunition from the bus, but it's all training bullets. We can't pierce armour with it, but we can still fight, and we can still train.

We train for two days, then Will sends us ten more volunteers, and we start again.

Will sources more paint for us, and we spray the first group's armour black, laying it out in the barn after a training session and checking each other's work, making sure it looks perfect. Jake and Amy bring their armour to the barn, and we spray that as well. We pack everything away in the morning, and spray another ten suits the next day. It's thrilling to be defacing so many of Commander Bracken's precious uniforms, and erasing the names from the front panels and helmets. Every time I paint over someone's name, it feels as if I am setting a recruit free. It feels good.

By the sixth day of training, I'm feeling triumphant. Including ourselves, we've got thirty people fitted with armour and trained to fire guns. We've disguised all the armour, and we've checked the radios and the contamination panels. We're building ourselves an army, and I'm excited to think that we might be able to make a difference.

Dan and I tidy the barn and follow the recruits back to the bunker. I have time to take a shower and change into clean clothes before dinner, and I find myself singing under the stream of hot water, and as I head back to my room. Charlie comes in while I'm tying my boots, and closes the door behind her.

"How are you doing?"

I laugh. "I'm great! I'm making a difference, I'm training people to fight the government. We stole all those crates of armour, and now we're making sure they get used. We've just bought ourselves a huge advantage, and now we can actually do something!"

Charlie looks concerned. She opens her mouth to speak, but there's a knock on the door, and Dan shouts about going to dinner. I straighten my T-shirt, open the door, and dance down the corridor, Dan and Charlie trailing behind me.

The dining room is quiet, and I wonder whether we're early for the meal, but Jo waves to us to sit down while she brings the food to our table. Amy and Saunders arrive with Jake, and Dr Richards comes in with Margie. We sit together and pass the food round the table, helping ourselves and catching up with what everyone has been doing. Jake and Amy have been filling Will in on the changes to procedures at camp after our escape. Jake still isn't speaking to me, but he's talkative enough with everyone else, and clearly happy to be here. Saunders has just woken up, and he's looking forward to his first night shift with the security guard. Dr Richards and Margie have been in the meeting room for most of the day, and they're happy to relax and laugh with the rest of us.

It is wonderful to feel safe and accepted by people who all want the same thing I do. I glance around the dining room, looking for our trainees, and feeling excited again about what we've managed to do.

But there's hardly anyone here. Jo and a few other people are at the table near the stove, and the other tables are empty. I can't see Will, or my trainees, anywhere.

My happy mood starts to fade, and I feel my stomach dropping.

"Where is everyone?"

My question interrupts the laughter and the chatter. Dr Richards and Margie exchange a look.

"Where's Will?"

"He's taken them on a mission," Dr Richards begins. "They're following some good intelligence, and they're going to disrupt a supply convoy."

I'm on my feet before I can think. "Why aren't we there? Why hasn't he taken us?"

Charlie puts her hand on my arm, but I shrug her off.

"I don't think he trusts us, Bex. Not after what we did on the coach." Dan sounds resigned, as if he agrees with Will.

"Did you know?" I'm angry now. He shakes his head.

"How are we supposed to fight back? How are we supposed to make a difference, if we can't fight?"

And everyone is talking at once, telling me I have made a difference, that I trained the fighters, that they couldn't do this without the armour. I push my plate away, throw my hands in the air, and walk out.

There's nowhere to go. I run up the stairs and pace the corridors until I've calmed down, then walk back down to my room and sit on my bed, my head in my hands.

There's a gentle knock on the door, and Charlie comes in. She sits on her bed, and waits for me to look at her. When I do, it's through tears.

"You know Will's right."

I shake my head. "You don't understand."

"Oh, I do. He's turned you into another front-line doll. You're allowed to go with him when the stakes are low, or when he doesn't have a choice, but you're not allowed to join his real army. You're not allowed to actually fight."

She's right. I got Will his armour, I took it from Ketty and Jackson. I got him the guns and the ammunition, and I trained his soldiers. I did all the things he asked me to do, and now I'm stuck in the bunker and he doesn't want me with him when the fighting gets real. It doesn't matter what I do – I'm always the PR exercise. I'm always the front-line doll.

None of this is real. The City Killers were real, the government power-grab is real. But the rebels? The fight-back? We're just scratching the surface. We can't make a difference – not in the numbers we have here.

"I don't think we can do this," I whisper. "I don't think we have enough people. I don't think we can fight them." I lie back, my head on my pillow, and stare at the ceiling.

Charlie takes a deep breath. "That might be true. And maybe you're always going to be a front-line doll. But I thought the point was that you're a front-line doll for the good guys."

I can't help laughing. "I guess that is better."

"You can't do everything. You can't win this war by yourself. You need to trust Will, and you need to do the things you're good at. You're really good at teaching people, Bex. You're really good at caring about people, and making sure the ones who are behind keep up with everyone else."

"I've got the bruises to show for it."

"I know you have. And that's one more reason to be working for the good guys. They value your input."

"I don't feel valued." But I know that isn't true. I know I'm playing an important role here. I just want the chance to show the people who killed a town that I know what they did. That I saw it, and that I won't let it stand.

"Come on, Bex. You know Will needs you. You just scared him, on the coach. You're a wild card, and he doesn't know you well enough to trust you yet."

There's another tap on the door, and Dan rushes in, followed by Margie. He's holding four cans of beer, and he hands them round as Margie sits on the end of my bed and Dan sits next to Charlie. He holds up his drink.

"To the mission."

"To the mission!"

Everyone else drinks, but I stay lying on my bed, holding my beer in one hand.

"They couldn't do this without you," says Margie, shaking my leg, "so cheer up, soldier!"

I prop myself up on one elbow, lifting my beer can. "How did you get these?"

Dan grins. "I told Jo it was an emergency. She made us the official rescue party! We can't lose you, Bex."

"So drink up!" Margie slaps my knee, and glares at me until I take a drink.

It's good to be back with my friends.

Silence

We talk for what seems like hours. I take off my boots and curl up under my blanket, and we tell Charlie stories about school. She tells us stories about Commander Bracken, and she laughs until she cries when we tell her about calling him Batman, and his assistant, Robin. Amy comes in, surprised to find us all here, and listens while we talk. I'm drifting in and out of the conversation, and I hardly notice when Margie stands up, picks up my beer can from the floor, and pulls the blanket up round my shoulders. I must have fallen asleep before everyone else went to bed.

I wake with my heart pounding. I'm terrified, and it takes me a moment to work out why. It's dark, and the light spilling under the door from the corridor is dimmer and paler than it should be. I sit up, and then I realise what has woken me.

Silence.

There's no sound. No air conditioning, no ventilation, no chatter from other rooms. I can hear Charlie and Amy breathing gently, but the quiet is oppressive. Something isn't right.

I carefully lift my blanket and swing my feet onto the floor. I stand, as quietly as I can, and tiptoe to the door. I open it a crack and look out into the corridor.

The strip lights that light the bunker day and night are off. The pale, blueish light is coming from the emergency torches, plugged in, three of them along each wall. They only light up if the power goes out, so we've lost our electricity supply. I step out, grab the closest torch from its holder, and retreat into my room. My kitchen crate of armour is under my bed, so I pull it out, change into base layers, and start clipping it on.

I freeze when I hear voices. I can't tell what they're saying, but I think the sound is carrying through the ventilation pipes. No one has tripped an alarm, but the power outage should have attracted some attention by now. One of the guards should have noticed.

There are more voices. I'm shaking off sleep, and I realise that this could be the start of an attack. I step over and shake Charlie's shoulder, then walk down the room and shake Amy awake, too.

"Get up!" I hiss, sounding impossibly loud in the silence.

I clip the last of the armour into place, and sit down to lace my boots. Amy sits up and I toss the torch on to the end of her bed.

"Get up, and get your armour on." She looks at me through hooded eyes, but gets up and starts dressing herself. Charlie stirs, and sees what I'm doing. She's up and pulling on her jeans in seconds.

"What's happened?"

"I don't know, but we've lost power. I don't like it."

Charlie reaches under her bed and grabs her duffel bag. She stuffs my trousers and T-shirt in on top of her clothes, and grabs Amy's fatigues from the end of her bed. She pushes her feet into her trainers, tightens the laces, and she's ready to go. Amy reaches under her pillow and silently pulls out a bundle of paper – sketches from Saunders. She carefully tucks them into the top of Charlie's bag, then pulls on her base layers. Charlie helps her put on her armour while I grab my helmet and gun, and creep back out into the corridor. I take two of the lit torches from their charging points, open the door to Dan's room, and slide them in along the floor.

"Get up! Get your armour on!" I wait until I see Dan start to sit up, and I back out of the room.

Charlie and Amy are behind me as we make our way along the corridor. I can still hear the voices, and noises like someone using a hammer or firing a gun, echoing along the ventilation ducts, but there is no one else around. I check the bathrooms and open the dormitory doors as we walk past, but all the beds are empty – this is where our trainees were sleeping. In the final room we find Jo, already getting dressed, and the other women from her table at dinner, rousing themselves and getting up.

"Grab the spare armour from the storeroom," she whispers, as we leave the room. "We'll be right behind you."

I don't know whether to be relieved or frightened that Jo is also assuming we're under attack.

We walk, slowly and quietly, to the end of the corridor. Dan is behind us now, and Jake is clipping the last pieces of his armour on as they catch up with us.

"Saunders?" I whisper.

Dan points upstairs. "On watch." And I remember his proud boast at dinner, that this would be his first night shift.

I take another torch from a wall socket, and gently push open the door to the hallway beyond.

There's no one here, and the emergency torches are all still in place. I wave everyone through, and send Dan to knock on the remaining bedroom doors, along the corridor to our right. I don't want to leave anyone behind.

We gather in the hallway at the bottom of the stairs. The voices have stopped now, and every movement we make seems impossibly loud. There's a ringing in my ears where the sound of the ventilation system should be, and I'm starting to panic at the thought of being trapped, three levels underground in a concrete bunker.

I motion everyone to stay still, and I start to climb the stairs, careful to make as little noise as I can. Halfway up, the flight of stairs doubles back on itself, and I lean round the corner to check what's ahead.

Emergency torchlight is lighting the next level up. I can't hear anyone ahead of us, but I'll have to go up and make sure. I twist my helmet onto my suit to free up my left hand, and open the visor. Stooping to keep my head below the level of the top step, I move slowly up the stairs.

There's no one on the second landing, so I retrace my steps to the turn in the staircase and beckon everyone up. Dan is back with two of the men who were at dinner with us, and Jo is here with the other women.

I head back up to the landing. There's a door ahead of me, and a door to my right. Both corridors are lit by emergency torches, and both are empty. This level houses the kitchen and common room to the right, and store rooms straight ahead. I raise my gun, and push the door ahead of me open.

Emergency torches still line the walls, and the store room doors are closed. Jo follows me through and heads for the second door. She takes a torch from the wall and disappears inside. I wave the others through, keeping Dan and Amy in the hallway. Charlie and the others will need a few minutes to get suited up. Dan and Amy walk the length of the corridor, opening store rooms and checking for anyone inside. I send Jake in to help assemble the armour, and then take off my gloves and head in myself.

I'm amazed by how calmly everyone is handling this situation. Everywhere I look, people who haven't been trained are pulling on base layers and helping each other to clip the armour together. If it's too big or too small, people are swapping crates and finding a size that works for them. I help out where I need to, and quietly remind everyone to make sure they have a helmet and a gun. I help several people with their helmets, and raise their visors so they can hear the noises around them. I point out the weak spots on the armour, and make sure people don't think they're invincible. A training bullet through the soft, movable sections will kill them just as quickly as an armour-piercing round anywhere else.

Jo pulls a crate from the back of the room and waves me over. It's the ammunition supply. Training bullets only, but it's better than nothing. I walk round the room, checking the magazine in every gun, and handing everyone a spare to clip to their waists. I take spares for myself, Dan, and Amy, and make my way back to the door. I open it and lean out. The corridor is empty. I pull my gloves back on, walk out, and wave everyone else to follow me.

We meet up with Dan and Amy in the hallway, and they clip their spare magazines to their armour. They've found no one else on this corridor. One more flight of stairs to go. I look around at the group we've assembled.

"Where's Margie? And Dr Richards?" Dan looks round at everyone, and shrugs.

We've checked all the dorms. I send Dan to check the kitchen and common room while I move slowly up the stairs to check the next hallway. My movements, my breathing, and the tiny movements of the people in the hallway below, are the only sounds. The hallway above is clear, and I head back down to beckon everyone up. Dan pushes through the group from the corridor, hands open and empty. There's no one else on this level.

We move up the stairs, and assemble in the final hallway. I wave Dan to check the meeting room and the offices, and Amy to check the workshops. They work their way along both corridors on this level, and return quickly, shaking their heads.

There's no one else in the bunker. There are fifteen of us, and only four with training for the guns and armour. The next stage is the most dangerous – we need to leave the living areas of the bunker and climb up to the gatehouse.

I gather everyone close to me, so I can talk quietly but everyone can hear me. I make sure everyone has their helmets on and clipped into their armour, and then I send Dan, Jake, and Amy to switch on all the suit radios, and make sure they are tuned to the same channel.

Charlie is standing next to me, and I turn to help her. I take her hand, and activate the radio with the controls on the back of the glove. I switch it to the right channel, and show her how to use the controls.

I'm watching as she presses the button with her right hand, and I notice that the contamination panel on her armour is different from mine. The display panels are smaller, and there's a grey panel at the end near the glove that I don't have. I lift her arm to check, and I see the light, flashing on and off, red against the grey plastic.

It takes me a moment to understand, and then I'm pushing through the group, grabbing people's arms and checking all the panels.

All the new suits of armour have smaller displays, and a tiny, flashing light.

My mind is racing. Maybe it's nothing. Maybe it's an upgrade to the contamination panels.

And maybe it's a tracker.

And suddenly everything makes sense. If we are under attack, it means the government has found us. They've been searching for so long – why have they suddenly tracked us down? I'm sure the signals can't escape from the bunker. The walls are too thick, and we're too far underground.

I think about the journey back from the raid on the coach. I know they didn't follow us, but they could have been tracking the trucks. And I think about the armour, in the barn. Spray-painted and left overnight to dry. Ten trackers every night, sending out their location for hours.

We've given ourselves away, and we've led the army right to us.

I smack my glove into the concrete wall of the hallway and cry out in frustration, and the sound is too loud in the quiet space.

"Bex?"

"They're trackers. The new contamination panels. They're trackers, so the government can find lost soldiers …"

"… and stolen armour." Dan sounds resigned. "That's how they've found us."

"Take them out. Take them all out."

We work our way round the group, unclipping the new panels and disconnecting them from the stolen suits.

I send Jake and Amy to leave the trackers in a pile under Amy's bed – the furthest point from the entrance to the bunker.

"You couldn't have known," Charlie says, her hand gentle on my shoulder.

"I should have spotted them earlier. I should have seen them when we unpacked the crates."

"They'd still have tracked us back to the farmhouse." Dan sounds as hopeless as I feel.

"Will was right! I've completely screwed up. No one should be trusting me." I slap the wall again, fighting tears.

Will. I realise that he's gone out with a team of people wearing trackers on their suits. There's no way they're getting away with their convoy attack, and there's no way they're getting back here without being caught. My knees give way underneath me, and I'm sitting on the floor, my head in my hands.

"But … Will's team's wearing the new armour." Charlie is making the connection as she speaks.

I nod. I can't speak. I have made this happen. I've brought the army here, and I've trained Will's team to fight with targets on their backs. We should never have come. We should never have broken Margie out of the camp.

"We need to get out. We need to get away before they come down here and find us." Dan grabs my arm as he speaks, dragging me to my feet. "We need to save ourselves."

I nod, and try to clear my thoughts. I need to focus on getting this group to safety.

"We're going to need supplies. We can't come back here." I turn to the group as Jake and Amy come running up the stairs. "Spread out. Grab a rucksack, grab the stuff that you're going to need, and then fill your bag up with ration bars and water. Quickly. Go!"

Charlie touches my arm. "Stay here, Bex. I'll pack you a bag." I nod, and she runs down the stairs.

I'm alone in the hallway. I feel winded, as if someone has punched me in the chest. I can't believe we've been broadcasting our location. How easy it was for the government to track our movements. That Will is out there now.

I need to concentrate.

Dan is the first person to come back with his bag packed, gun in hand. He looks at me, puts his gun down and gives me a tight, crushing hug. "We can do this. We can get out of here."

He holds me for a long time, and eventually I hug him back.

The others start to arrive, rucksacks on their backs. Charlie is the last to return. She hands my bag to me, and I unclip my gun and shrug the rucksack onto my shoulders.

"We're going to get out of the bunker. When we do, I need all of you to disappear into the forest. Run, hide, make your way to the lake. We'll meet up there, on the far side.

"Visors down, radios on." There's the sound of visors clicking into place, and radios activating. I close my visor, switch my radio on. "Can everyone hear me?" There's a jumble of voices in my ear. "Raise your hand if you can hear." Fourteen hands are lifted. "Let's go."

Reality

The door to the final staircase is the armoured door protecting the bunker. The locking mechanism is a wheel, like the doors on submarines, and the door is made of heavy, thick metal.

Dan and I grab the wheel and turn it, jumping at every squeak and clang it makes as it moves. The door swings open towards us, and I signal everyone else to stay back.

The stairwell, with its metal steps, is dark. Dan hands me one of the emergency torches, and I point it upwards, into the black. The space is empty, but the stairs will be loud under our feet. We can't afford to be caught at this stage – this is a choke point, and there's no other way out.

I tell Dan to stay with the group, and I start to make my way, as quietly as possible, up the steps.

It is impossible to stay silent on the metal stairs. The staircase doubles back on itself three times before ending in a landing, and the door to the gatehouse. I creep up, each step as gentle and quiet as I can make it, but the sound is unbearably loud, even through my helmet.

The door at the top is closed. I take a deep breath, and turn the handle. The door opens, but I'm trying to understand why I can't see anything, when I realise there's a security shutter sealing me inside the stairwell.

I call Dan up, and he makes the same agonising climb, keeping every movement as slow and gentle as possible. I can feel the staircase shaking as he makes each step.

I shine my torch onto the shutter. "We're sealed in."

Dan pushes the shutter, but it hardly moves. "We are. There must be some controls on this side."

We start looking. "If we're lucky, they won't be powered by the main bunker supply."

There's a metal box behind the door, but the button on the front does nothing. Dan steps round the door, and starts pulling on the cover of the box. I stand back and let him work.

The cover comes free, and inside there's a handle – a lever we can turn. I kneel down on the top step, and Dan starts to turn the lever. The shutter starts to move.

The noise seems deafening in the silence, but Dan keeps turning, and I put my head on the floor and look out into the entrance hall.

The lights are on, blindingly bright; and the screens – although I can't see the images clearly from here. As the shutter creeps upwards, I see someone lying on the floor, and an overturned chair next to the screens. The door to the outside is closed, and there's no one else in the space. I signal to Dan to move faster, and the shutter rises into the doorframe.

I step out into the room, gun raised. The screens are showing grainy, night-time images from the farmyard, and I can't see them clearly from across the room.

What I can see is Saunders, lying beside his chair, face towards me, eyes lifeless. There's a dark red stain across the front of his T-shirt and on the floor around him.

I hurry over and kneel beside him, calling his name. I shake his shoulder. I pull off my glove and check his neck for a pulse, but there's nothing. I'm pushing on his neck, willing his heart to beat, but I know he's gone. His skin is too cold, and his eyes stare past me. I slide my hand under his head, cradle it in my hands.

"I'm sorry. I'm so, so sorry!"

I'm expecting tears, but instead I feel a cold determination building in my chest, like an iceberg. This is something else I will not let them do without a fight. My own heartbeat is roaring in my ears.

There are voices on the radio, and I realise that everyone can hear me. Gently, I lay Saunders down on the cold floor, and close his eyes. His sketch of all of us, from the camp, is lying on the floor next to him. Without thinking I pick it up and tuck it into my belt. I kneel next to him for a moment, and focus on breathing slowly. I'm suddenly seeing his face, at dinner only hours ago; his pride at taking his first night shift in the gatehouse.

There should be a security guard with him, but there's no one else here. Slowly I get to my feet and step over Saunders, looking at the screens.

Dan's voice cuts through my thoughts. "Bex! I'm bringing them up."

I murmur something positive. I'm looking at the screens. It's dark outside – the CCTV footage claims it's three o'clock in the morning – but the farmyard is brightly lit. There are floodlights on the barn and on the outbuildings, and someone has switched them all on. There are two armoured troop carriers blocking the yard off from the driveway, and in the middle of the farmyard, two people are on their knees, soldiers standing behind them holding guns.

I lean in, closer to the screens.

It's Margie and Dr Richards.

There's a shouted conversation going on. Someone out of sight near the farmhouse is shouting at the soldiers, and they're shouting and gesturing back. I look at the other screens, but the figure is in darkness. There's no sound with the images, but it is clear that this is an argument.

There's a thundering sound from the staircase as someone sprints up the final flight of stairs. I hear a cry as they stumble through the door, and I glance back to see Amy, visor up, shaking her head, one hand over her mouth, one hand reaching out to where Saunders is lying on the floor. Jo follows her through the door and gently takes her elbow, guiding her to his side. Amy kneels and takes his hand in hers. She leans forward and rests her head on his chest, one hand gripping the neck of his T-shirt, shaking him as if she's trying to wake him. She reaches out and strokes his hair, sobbing quietly.

I can feel the anger building in my chest, the iceberg sending cold determination through my body. I want to scream and shout, but I need to focus. I need to get everyone away. We're trapped by our own defences, and we need to get out of this tiny concrete box. I need to understand what's happening outside.

Dan steps up and stands beside me, and the others begin to follow him into the room. He points at the images from the farmyard.

"Is that …?"

I nod, my fists clenched, watching my friends on the screens. I want to fight back. I want to keep everyone safe. I can't lose anyone else today.

"Get the others out."

Dan stands, watching me.

"Get them out!"

And this time I'm screaming.

Dan nods, steps over to the door, and cracks it open. There's no gunfire, no sound of approaching soldiers, so he opens it further and steps outside. The footsteps on the stairs have stopped, and the gatehouse is crowded now, but quiet. No one moves.

One gunshot. Two. Just outside the bunker. Without thinking, I bring my gun up and aim it at the door.

"Dan …"

There's a cry, quickly stifled, from Amy, then silence. I wave everyone else back as I move to cover the doorway. I'm surprised and grateful when Jake steps up next to me, gun levelled. I think about Dan, outside in the dark, dead or alive. I think about Amy tucking her sketches into Charlie's bag. I think about Saunders. I think about who might be coming through the door.

And then he's back. Dan's back, his visor up and his face pale, opening the door and beckoning everyone else to leave. He's holding two extra guns, taken from the guards outside. I let my arms fall to my sides, take a deep breath, and try to stop my hands shaking as I step out of the way, past Saunders and Amy to the screens.

"How …?" Jake steps over to Dan, lowering his gun.

"Soft spots on the armour. Took them by surprise, point-blank." Dan sounds breathless. He points at his shoulder and under his arm, his hands shaking.

He holds up a gun. "Armour-piercing bullets. Take this, and make sure everyone makes it." He hands the gun and a spare magazine to Jake, then turns to the rest of us. "Watch your step. Meet up at the lake. Be quick and be quiet!"

He ushers our companions out of the bunker. There are murmurs of assent as the group leaves the gatehouse and dissolves into the darkness of the forest. I glance at the door, and see Jo helping Amy to walk out into the night. She looks back at Saunders, silent tears staining her face, and my determination grows.

I concentrate on the feed from the farmyard. On the screens the soldiers are still arguing, and their prisoners are watching, waiting to see what will happen.

I turn back, to find Dan and Charlie waiting for me, visors raised.

"What are you doing? Go!"

They both shake their heads.

"You're about to do something stupid, Bex. We're here to make sure you survive."

Confrontation

Visors down, guns up, we leave the gatehouse. We switch off the lights, crack open the door, and step out into the dark. Two shapes in black armour lie slumped on the ground outside, dropped by Dan's bullets at point-blank range. I step over them, careful not to trip in the dark. Ahead of us, the farmhouse is a silhouette against the floodlights in the yard, and above us shafts of light shine through the tops of the trees. Against the bright light, the back of the farmhouse is invisible – we can't tell whether there are guards waiting for us.

We've switched our radios to a private channel, just the three of us. We make our way along the path to the back of the house, every step cushioned by the carpet of pine needles. At the back door, I risk using my torch, flashing it quickly left and right to make sure there's no one waiting in the shadows. Through the window, I can see torch beams moving inside the house, but out here we're alone.

Dan moves left, and I move right, along the back of the house. We're aiming for the yard, at opposite ends of the building. Charlie stays near the back door as our lookout – she hasn't been trained in using the gun, and while we've shown her how to fire it, she won't be much use in the open.

I reach the corner of the house, and risk a glance round the corner towards the barn. The end of the house and the side of the barn are in shadow, but I can see the end of the farmyard under the floodlights.

There's no one in sight.

"Sit tight, Charlie."

"Be safe, Bex."

I step out, keeping close to the wall, and move carefully towards the yard. Through my helmet, I can hear shouting. I crack open my visor and listen.

Someone is shouting at Margie and Dr Richards, demanding to know where the terrorists are hiding. Dr Richards calmly explains that she doesn't know what they are talking about. Her voice is steady and clear, and I'm amazed that she can sound so calm, surrounded by soldiers. The shouting begins again, and she replies again, refusing to be intimidated. I realise that this conversation must have been going on for some time, and that the interrogator is barely controlling his anger.

I reach the end of the farmhouse wall. I need to be able to see into the yard, and I can't do that from here without putting myself into the light.

"Dan. Stay in the shadows. I'm going to use the barn for cover."

"Understood. Plenty of shadows this end of the yard."

"Can you see Margie?"

"Not yet."

I retrace my steps to the back corner of the house, and then use the trees for cover as I skirt round to the back of the barn. There's a little light here, but I'm still in shadow, and I can see into the yard.

Dr Richards is on her knees, a soldier in fatigues behind her with a gun in one hand, and the other hand on her shoulder. Margie is kneeling close by, hands behind her back, a soldier standing guard.

I can hear shouting, and I can see a shadow on the ground as someone paces round the yard, shouting his questions.

He steps past Margie, into the light. It's Commander Bracken.

"Bex! Are you seeing this?" Dan sounds breathless.

"Yes." My throat is tight. I watch the Commander step over to Margie and pull her head back by her hair.

"Do you know where they are?"

Margie doesn't move. Dr Richards stares straight ahead.

My heart is thumping.

"Where are the other soldiers?" I whisper. I can only see a small part of the yard, but I can't see anyone else. There are people inside the farmhouse, but no more guards.

"There's a couple at the front of the barn, but that's it. Four, that I can see, plus Commander Bracken."

I look back, into the trees, but I can't see anyone else.

Then there's the noise of an engine, approaching on the drive.

"Get away from the driveway, Dan. We've got company."

"I'm already moving." I can hear from his voice that he's running.

The engine noise gets louder. Commander Bracken drops Margie's hair, and waves over the two guards from the front of the barn. They're wearing black armour, like the troops I saw in town. Like the armour I'm wearing. He sends one to the driveway, and one into the house, then stands in front of Dr Richards, as if he expects her to break down and tell him everything. She stares past him, saying nothing.

The engine noise grows to a roar, and then dies. At the far end of the yard, behind the troop carriers, the guard walks up to what looks like a small fuel tanker.

I want to storm the yard. I want to grab Dr Richards and Margie while the guards are distracted. I want to put my gun to Commander Bracken's head.

The door to the farmhouse opens, and a line of guards files out, all wearing black armour. I count ten, plus the one who went inside to fetch them.

"Nothing, Sir," says the first guard.

"You've searched?"

"Everywhere. There's no one here."

The Commander leans down and grabs Dr Richards by her chin, forcing her to look up at him.

"Anything to say?"

"I've told you. There's no one else here." Cool, calm, controlled. He lets go, and turns to the guards.

"Stage Two. Get set up."

The guards run past the troop carriers to the tanker, out of sight.

"Dan! Where are you?"

"I'm in the shadows, Bex. I'm trying to see what they're doing."

The Commander is pacing again.

There's a shout from behind the house, back in the woods.

"There's activity here." Charlie's voice, sounding nervous.

"What's happening?"

"There are people coming, along the path from the bunker."

"Get into the trees, Charlie! Go! Now!" Dan's voice.

"Going."

"Dan, talk to me. What can you see?"

"Not much. I'm right back in the trees. There's a pipe coming from the back of the tanker – like a fireman's hose. They're adding new sections to it, and they're bringing it this way."

"Stay down. Keep out of sight. Charlie – are you safe?"

"In the trees. I don't think anyone saw me. There's a crowd of people coming your way."

I retreat towards the far end of the barn, keeping low and staying out of sight.

There's movement along the wall of the farmhouse, and a line of soldiers in black armour jogs into the flood-lit yard. Twenty or so soldiers, helmets on, guns on their backs. One of them flips his visor up, and speaks to Commander Bracken. It's too quiet for me to hear, but the Commander nods, and sends him over to the tanker.

The other soldiers gather next to the farmhouse. I risk stepping out from the barn to get a better view of the yard.

Nineteen or twenty soldiers in armour. Two in fatigues, plus the Commander. Two prisoners. And the team at the tanker.

Can I do it? Can I get into the yard and shoot the soldiers in fatigues? I think it through. I know I can get in, but I'm equally sure that I can't get out again. Whatever I do in the yard, that's it for me, and probably for Margie and Dr Richards as well.

I tap my fist against the barn, as hard as I dare. We've missed our chance. I've screwed up again.

"Oh, god!" It's Charlie. I crouch down against the wall. "Are you OK? Are you OK? Oh, god – talk to me!"

"Charlie? What's happening?"

"Sorry – Bex, I've found someone. I've found the guard from the bunker."

Saunders' partner on the night shift. She keeps talking to the guard, and I can't hear his response.

"Charlie?"

"He's hurt. He says they forced their way into the gatehouse, and demanded to know what was behind the shutter. But he wouldn't tell them. They cut the power, but they didn't know that the gatehouse has battery backup. They were surprised to find anyone there."

I'm breathing fast, and all I can see is Saunders, lying on the gatehouse floor.

"He was waiting for them with one of Will's rifles, but the bullets just bounced off their armour. They asked about the shutter, and when he wouldn't talk they shot him, they shot Saunders, and they left. The guard made it outside, but he had to hide in the trees. There were soldiers walking up and down the path with torches and crates." There's a pause, while she whispers something to the guard.

"He's bleeding, Bex. It's bad."

"Where were the soldiers going?" I wait while she relays the question.

"He doesn't know. Somewhere back in the woods. I think they're the group who just came back."

Soldiers in the woods. The tanker. Commander Bracken's frustration. What's his plan? What's Stage Two?

"Dan. Can you get to Charlie?"

"I'll try."

"Stay out of sight. What's happening at the tanker?"

"They're adding more sections to the hose. They're bringing it round to the back of the house."

For a moment I imagine them flooding the house with petrol and burning it down – but what would that achieve? And what's in the woods? Are they targeting the lake? For a minute I panic that everyone who escaped with us will be caught as they wait for us to arrive. I didn't think the soldiers would get that far. I close my eyes, breathe deeply, and concentrate.

And then all the lights in the house come on at once. It's dazzling, and suddenly there's no shadow on this side of the barn. I edge my way round the corner, and crouch against the back wall. I can't see anything happening in the yard, and neither can Dan. We're cut off from Margie and Dr Richards, and I can't see what the soldiers are doing.

With the lights comes the sound of a boiler, kicking in as the power returns. Someone has restored power to the farmhouse. Have they powered up the bunker as well? Can they move the shutter? Or are they planning on using something else?

I remember the silence that woke me. The ringing in my ears where the sound of the ventilation system should be.

"Charlie! Where's the intake for the ventilation system? Where does the bunker get its air?"

She repeats my question for the guard.

"Out in the woods. Near the lake."

So they've found the bunker. They think we're all inside, and they're going to poison the air.

I almost laugh out loud. All this time and effort, to poison an empty bunker. And I realise they didn't know the bunker was here. They thought the farmhouse was the base – no wonder they've searched it so thoroughly. Dr Richards and Margie must have been in the farmhouse when they raided it, sleeping there while Will and the guards are away. It must have been a surprise to find Saunders and the guard, with their bank of screens, watching everything they were doing. While we were getting out, they were looking for clues, and they must have found the ventilation pipes. Figured out that there's a bunker under the gatehouse.

I realise that the commander wasn't asking for information from his prisoners. He was pushing them for a confession. That would make a death sentence inevitable for both of them.

The armour trackers will have confirmed everything. The signals disappeared when we brought them here, and then reappeared in the barn overnight. They must have realised the armour was being stored somewhere that blocked the signals.

And now they're getting ready to gas us all in our sleep.

Let them. We don't need to stop them. We need to get our friends back.

I lean carefully round the side of the barn. The prisoners are on their feet, hands behind their backs. The guards are holding them still, gripping their arms. Commander Bracken is talking with one of the soldiers in armour, gesturing towards the vehicles and the tanker. The other soldiers are standing in small groups, visors up, waiting for orders.

If I can get myself into the yard, I'll be able to get close to the guards. They probably won't notice another suit of armour, and if I can get close enough, I can grab one of the prisoners. Maybe both. After that, I'm relying on confusion to protect us while we get away.

I don't have time to think this through. I've got one chance.

"Dan – you know that stupid thing I'm going to do? I'm doing it now. Get yourselves to the lake – I'll meet you there."

"Bex –"

"Go! I'll see you there."

I pull my visor down and stand up. I can feel the adrenaline pushing me to run, pushing me to act without hesitating. I slow my breathing, and force myself to walk round the barn, and out into the yard.

I'm right. No one sees me. I'm behind the guards, and no one is looking in my direction. I slow my pace to a brisk walk, and approach the first guard. I reach out as I pass, and take Dr Richards from him. I take her arm in my hand and I walk past. He lets go in surprise, and I keep walking. Dr Richards struggles in my grasp, I slip my arm through hers, and she looks at me in surprise. She can't see me through the visor. I transfer my gun to the hand on her side, walk over to the other guard, and I'm about to grab Margie when the first guard shouts.

In slow motion, I see my hand reaching out, closing round Margie's arm – but her arm moves. The guard pulls her away, and my fist closes on nothing. Dr Richards shouts as the guard throws Margie to the ground and turns his gun towards me. I look behind me. Commander Bracken is running towards us, and the other guard is raising his gun.

The Commander is shouting orders, pointing past me at the tanker crew. As I turn back I see the soldiers in armour dropping their visors and reaching for something at their waists. There's activity at the back of the tanker. The guards are shouting, and running with the Commander towards the troop carriers. Margie crawls to her feet, tripping as she tries to stand, and Dr Richards twists out of my grip and runs to help her.

Everyone is running to the vehicles, and I'm still trying to understand what's happening. Someone has turned a tap at the back of the tanker, and there's a spreading puddle of liquid on the ground. Tendrils of grey mist are creeping across the farmyard from the driveway. Margie is coughing and trying to run. Dr Richards pulls her sweater up over her mouth and nose and pulls Margie with her. The guards catch up with them and pull them towards the troop carriers.

And then it's if someone has struck the back of my head with a hammer. Someone behind me is firing their gun. My neck snaps forward as the bullet grazes my helmet, and I'm running as well. Another bullet thumps into the ground in front of me. The next shot could bring me down. I keep running. I need to get out of the yard.

Commander Bracken is throwing camouflaged bags out of the nearest vehicle. He tears one of them open, and pulls a gas mask down over his face. He opens another and hands it to Margie, and another to her guard. The mist is filling the farmyard, creeping along the ground and drifting into the air. I focus on running, past the vehicles, past the end of the house and into the woods beyond. Automatically, I check my contamination panel. The chemical section is turning red, and the level is climbing.

Bullets are snapping past me. The soldiers behind me don't need gas masks – their helmets are protecting them. As I run, I reach for the canister at my waist and activate my own air supply. I sprint for the end of the yard and turn past the corner of the house, into the deep shadow at the edge of the floodlights. The soldiers are right behind me, but I'm wearing black, and their eyes are used to the light. As quickly as I turned left, I turn right and run for the trees. I leap over the pipe, disconnected from the back of the tanker.

As I reach the undergrowth I can hear bullets impacting on the ground behind me. There's a pause in the firing as they realise that I'm not hiding near the house, and then the bullets are ripping through the trees around me. I dodge between the pines, putting as many tree trunks as possible between myself and the guns. The light from the yard is fading, and I'm running into blackness, my arms outstretched to stop me running into the trees.

I need to shake off the soldiers, and I need to get to the lake.

"Charlie! Dan! Turn your air supplies on and check the contamination level." I'm running, and my voice jumps as my feet hit the ground.

The guns behind me are slowing. Only a few bullets are reaching this deep into the trees, and eventually they stop altogether. I want to stop, catch my breath, but I can't. I need to get away. I turn back, and I see torch beams, heading away from me in the woods. The soldiers are heading back to the farmyard. I wait to see whether they are searching for me, but they keep walking, back towards the light.

I bend over, rest my hands on my knees and take a few deep breaths.

Their torchlight is fading, and I risk taking my torch from my waist and, keeping the beam low, switch it on. I wave it across the trees in front of me, and I feel myself begin to panic. Everything looks the same. A carpet of dried pine needles. Tree trunks. Dense branches in every direction. I need to keep moving, and I need to move away from the yard. I look back, locate the glow from the floodlights, turn round, and keep walking.

There's no team here – I'm on my own. I need to solve my own problems. Get myself out of danger.

I think of Saunders, his ankle twisted in the woods. I think of Amy, terrified on the assault course. I think of Margie, in the farmyard. Margie who I couldn't help.

I've made a mess. I've helped people, and I've been punished for it. I've tried to help my friends, and they'll be punished for my efforts. I've taken Margie from one prison cell to another, and I've handed Dr Richards to the government as well.

I let out a scream of frustration.

"Bex – are you … is that your torch?"

I stop. Can Dan see me? Slowly, I put my hand over the bulb, and then pull it away. Cover the light, uncover.

And there's another torch beam, off to my left. On, off. On, off.

"I see you!"

I walk towards the light, closing the space between us.

Reunion

We walk together to the lake, keeping our torch beams low. The contamination panels are clearing, and we're back on the path. Charlie and Dan are supporting the guard between them. They've tied a wet T-shirt round his face to protect him from the gas – it's not enough, but the contamination levels are lower out here, away from the farmyard. I'm on watch, keeping my gun ready, checking that we're not being followed.

We pass the ventilation pipes, hidden in a wooden box, about the size of a rabbit hutch. Crates and equipment are scattered across the path, and they were obviously planning to connect the pipe from the tanker to the air intake. Let them. There's no one in there for them to hurt now.

At the lake we switch our radios back to the group channel, and there's a welcome rush of voices. My contamination panel shows a pale shade of pink, getting paler all the time. I raise my visor as we walk into the group, gathered in the trees. I'm amazed to find that everyone's here. We've all made it out.

All except Saunders.

Charlie and Dan lower the guard to the ground and prop him against a tree. I want to join him, to sit down and let the night's events flow away from me. But we need to keep moving. We need to be away from here before daylight gives away our escape.

There's a smudge of light in the sky to the east, and we're running out of time to get ourselves away from Will's land. The soldiers will search for us when the light returns, and we need to be far away.

I give everyone a few minutes to collect their equipment – bags, guns, and helmets – and then I start to walk. I have no destination in mind – no plan – I just know that we can't stay here. The group follows, taking it in turns to help the injured guard. Charlie pulls the sketches out of her bag, gives them to Amy, and wraps her in a tight hug. They walk together, and Amy stumbles over the rough ground, unseeing, Jake's arm supporting her, Saunders' artwork in her hand.

"What happened back there?" whispers Dan, as we walk at the edge of the group.

"I screwed up."

"And Margie?"

"Alive. But the government has her. And Dr Richards."

He puts his arm round my shoulders and gives me a squeeze.

"You did your best, Bex. And you got all of us out." He waves his hand at the people walking with us.

"It wasn't enough."

"It's enough for today."

Walking

We've been walking for days. We've slept in out-buildings, in barns, under bridges. Everywhere, we've stayed out of sight. We've swapped our armour for civilian clothes, and our bags are full of plastic panels, unclipped and hidden away. We split up to walk through towns, and meet up again on deserted roads. We're trying to put as much space as possible between us and the farm. I don't know how long we'll walk for, or when we will be able to stop, but every day I feel happier that we are alive, and that we've come this far.

I let Saunders down, and I lost Margie and Dr Richards. I see their faces every time I close my eyes. I can't fix everything, but the people walking with me are alive because I brought them here.

I pull Saunders' sketch from my pocket. Apart from him, we're all safe. Apart from him, we're all still walking.

And maybe Dan's right. Maybe that's enough for today.

**False Flag
(Battle Ground #2)
is available now from Amazon
and all good bookshops.**

Keep reading for a preview!

KETTY

JUNE

Chapter 1: Newbies

They've been marching for days, these kids. They're scruffy and smelly and dirty. No one's taught them how to march, and they look as if they've never taken a shower or seen a washing machine. Would it kill them to use soap? Or a hairbrush?

They file into the camp, dead on their feet. Have they done any exercise in their lives? The newbies usually look exhausted, but these are beyond that. They're a disgrace.

Commander Bracken sent Jackson and Miller to meet them, and parade them in along the bypass. If it had been up to me, I'd have hidden them away and brought them in the back way, along the lanes. But it's not up to me, and here we are. I'm sure the good citizens of Leominster feel much safer, now that they've seen the urchins who are supposed to be protecting them.

There are some posh kids in this group, from some expensive boarding school up north. Kids with expectations that the world will be kind to them, and bow to their needs. It will be a pleasure to teach them the truth.

Jackson leaves the new arrivals with the camp staff and walks back to the Senior Dorm. He finds me at my table next to the window, finishing the commander's paperwork for this evening. He sits down opposite me.

"Did you see that?"

I sit back in my chair, arms folded. "I did. You two just marched that crowd of grubby civilian children past all the cars on the bypass. Feeling proud, are you?"

He ignores my grin.

"They're going to be tough to train, these kids. They didn't sign up. They don't know what's coming."

"Neither do the volunteers."

"No, but these recruits are soft. They don't want to be here. It's going to be hard, getting them up to fighting standard. Bracken isn't going to cut us any slack. We're the ones who'll need to put the pressure on, and we're the ones who'll get the blame when the kids can't handle the training."

He's right. I can mock them, and I can entertain myself with their incompetence, but I'm the one who needs to impress the commander. I need them to shape up fast, or it's my promotion that goes to someone else.

"No mercy, then. Whatever it takes to get them trained and ready, we do. Right?"

"Right", says Jackson, a wicked grin creeping across his face. "I won't report you, if you don't report me. Iron fists and steel toe caps. Deal?"

"Deal." Sounds good to me.

*****

After dinner, we head to the new recruits' dorm, and hang around outside the dining room. The camp staff are setting up their uniform distribution tables, and Commander Bracken is giving his usual speech. Jackson and I can do it by heart.

"Things I do not wish to see: dirty uniforms; torn uniforms; damaged uniforms; disrespected uniforms!"

We keep our voices down, sing-songing along with him, and watching the recruits we can see from the corridor.

They are pitiful. They are struggling to even stay awake. One hot meal and they think it's time for bed. Are they expecting a cup of warm milk and a bedtime story?

And then it happens. One of the recruits falls asleep at his table. We're watching from the corridor, and it is delicious. He's tiny, this kid. Hair all over the place, scuffed shoes, dangling shoelaces. His head drops, and he actually starts snoring! Snoring, while the commander is talking.

Jackson and I are smothering our laughter, making sure we're not overheard. We should walk away, but we're not missing this for anything.

Commander Bracken stops his speech, and looks at Assistant Woods. There's the flicker of a smile on Woods' face, and he walks over to the sleeping recruit and crashes his clipboard down on the table. I think the recruit is going to hit the ceiling. He wakes up in a hurry, and gets a fearsome earful from Woods.

I'm biting my knuckles so as not to make a noise, but this is the best entertainment we've had in weeks. Jackson is actually doubled over, gasping for breath, and now I'm laughing at both of them.

The commander picks up his speech again. The sleeping kid is shaking, and the others have a new look of terror on their faces. Good. They're going to need that.

The commander is reaching the end of his speech, and the kids are going to start leaving with their uniforms. We need to get out of the corridor.

As we're walking away, the commander addresses the sleeping kid.

"Saunders!"

"Sir!"

"You will stand where you are until the other recruits have their uniforms. When the last of your colleagues has left, then you may collect your uniform."

Jackson and I look at each other.

"So Saunders is the new whipping boy?"

He nods. "Saunders is the new whipping boy. Let's see how long it takes to put him in the hospital, as an example to the others."

I smile. "I'm going to enjoy this."

*****

When we arrived at camp, we all wanted to be here. We were fit, we were clean, we were eager to get started. We were fighters, and we wanted to be trained. We wanted to get better.

I signed up as soon as they'd let me. It was a ticket out of a dead-end job, and a ticket out of home as well. At the camp, life was simple. Do as you're told, keep fit, don't let them see you breaking the rules – and things would go well for you. You could earn promotions, special treatment, new opportunities. Screw up, get lazy, do something stupid, and expect punishment.

Justice.

It made a change from being punished because your Dad was drunk, or because he'd gambled away the housekeeping money. It made a change from apology gifts that he couldn't afford, and the anger that followed. At camp, there would always be enough food. Clothes to wear. Enough hot water in the pipes. And protection from the fists and boots of the person who was supposed to be your protector.

I have no idea what he's doing now. He's probably been evicted from the house. Without the income I kept hidden, he won't have been paying the rent. Too bad. You need discipline and determination and backbone to get anywhere in life, and he had none of those things. If he's on the street, he deserves it.

And I'm here. I'm doing fine without him. I'm going to get my promotion, and I'm getting out of here, too. If training these disastrous recruits is the price, bring it on. I'm ready.

Chapter 2: Disappointment

This is going to be harder than we imagined.

These kids are hopeless. Miller took them out for a run, and they've come back looking like the last people left alive after some terrible disaster. They're still standing, but their eyes are begging for the chance to rest and cuddle a blankie. It's the morning run! They need to do this every day. They have no idea what the weeks ahead have in store for them.

Day one, and they're already getting their hands on the guns. Command must be desperate. And I'm the one who gets to introduce them to weapons they are nowhere near being able to use.

Miller lines them up, and leaves me to run their first training session. I walk out in front of them, holding up the gorgeous rifle. There's no way they should be touching these yet, but here we are.

"Can anyone tell me what this is?"

Absolute silence.

"Come on. Anybody."

No one says a word. They're all trying to look invisible. Standing up straight and fading into the group. I look them over.

And there he is. Saunders, the whipping boy. In the front row, begging the universe to make me look the other way. He's out of luck.

"Saunders! Mr Sleepy himself. Can you tell me what this is?"

"A gun, Sir." His voice is shaking, and it's practically a whisper. Some people make such easy targets.

"Louder, Saunders!"

There's a pause, while he takes a deep breath. "A gun, Sir!"

"Thank you, Saunders." That's confused him. He's braced for more, but I turn away to address the group. Keep him guessing what's coming next.

"This is a gun. But this is not any gun. This is a prototype next-gen power-assisted rifle, firing armour-piercing bullets."

And you don't deserve to be playing with it.

"Under normal conditions, you lot wouldn't get to see one of these until you'd been training for years, if ever. You'd have to pass tests, and show that you're big enough to use one of these. But these aren't normal circumstances. This is war, and this is war on our home territory, and the decision makers have decided to let you worms loose with their favourite toys."

Several of the recruits wince at being called worms. At least they're listening.

"You'll be starting off with training bullets. We'll see how good you are, and whether you deserve to progress to armour-piercing rounds. Don't be fooled – training bullets will still kill you, so don't be stupid."

And don't get in my way.

"Make no mistake. You are getting your paws on these because the government wants to see them in use. The people in charge, they want you out there, waving these around to show Joe Public that we're protecting him."

And lucky me – I'm the one who has to train you to impress Joe Public.

"This isn't about you. This is about public confidence. About stopping panic and protecting people from themselves. While they can see you, and your guns, they'll be happy to get on with their lives and leave us to get on with ours."

If I can train you up in time.

I can't see any of these kids inspiring confidence, with or without deadly weapons.

"You are not fighting this war. We have a real army for that. You are showing the people that the war is being fought. You are the government's action figures. The front-line dolls. And public-facing dolls get the best weapons."

They don't like being called dolls. There are several scowls on the faces in front of me. I make a mental note to make sure they are clear on this point.

I switch my attention back to the whipping boy. His eyes widen as he realises that this isn't over.

"Saunders! Step out here."

He slouches out from the line of recruits, still willing the universe to ignore him. He's making it so easy for me to get them all quaking in their shiny new boots.

"Stand up straight, Saunders!"

He twitches his backbone a little. His shoulders still sag, and he looks as if he'd like the ground to swallow him up.

"Straighter! You're the line between life and messy death for those civilians out there. Try looking as if you could protect them from a bomber."

He straightens his shoulders, and I realise that he really is trying. This is honestly the best that he can do. I roll my eyes and shake my head. We have some long, torturous months ahead of us.

"It's like working with fluffy kittens. Grow some backbone, recruits!"

"Sir!"

He gives it his best shot, and it's a big improvement.

"Better. Now, Saunders. At ease. I'm going to hand you the gun. Show me how you'll be holding it when you're on patrol."

He stands clumsily at ease, and puts his hands out to take the gun. He looks terrified. His grip is hopeless, and he moves his hands along the barrel, trying to figure out how to hold it. I'm about to grab his hands and put them in the right places, when he seems to get it. He grasps the pistol grip firmly, and cradles the barrel with the other hand. His sudden confidence takes me by surprise.

"Not bad, recruit. Not bad."

I take his hands and correct his grip, just enough to make him doubt his own ability. His fingers are ink-stained, and his fingernails are chewed. He watches everything I do, making sure he knows how to get it right next time. His quick, shallow breathing is close to panic.

I take his shoulders and turn him round to face the group. He really is tiny, compared to the rest of them. Tiny, and fragile.

"This is a good grip. Watch and learn!"

Miller and Jackson and the other Senior Recruits are waiting as I spilt the kids into teams. I assign each team a Senior Recruit and a gun, and take the last team myself. The fluffy kittens follow every move as I show them how to take the rifle apart, clean it, maintain it and rebuild it.

As I work, I teach them the mantra.

"Safety on. Unclip the magazine, put it down. Unclip the pistol grip. Slide the handguard off the barrel, unscrew the barrel from the gun. Slide the stock up and away from the central section. Slide and unclip the elements of the central section. Lay them out neatly on the table."

I demonstrate several times, taking the gun apart, laying out the individual pieces, putting them back together. Some of the kids are whispering the mantra, desperate to memorise the actions.

I let them have a go. And it's all I can do not to laugh.

There's the kid who gets everything in the wrong order. There's the kid who knows the mantra, but can't make his hands stop shaking to take the gun apart. There's the smart kid who thinks she knows what she's doing, but forgets to clip the stock back into the gun before she attaches the pistol grip.

It's like watching a troupe of clowns.

Every time they get something wrong, I shout a little louder. By the end of the session, they're all shaking, and they all know how much they have to learn.

The whistle sounds for lunch. I call the recruits back into lines, and make sure they know how disappointed I am.

"That was pathetic! None of you is capable of handling a gun. None of you is competent enough to maintain a gun. None of you should be anywhere near a gun."

And if I had anything to do with it, you wouldn't be.

"But the commander wants you out there, looking competent and scary. And to be scary, you need guns. We will train, and train, and practice, and practice until every last one of you can handle a gun. Maintain, clean, hold, and use a gun. Look after your own gun, and look as if you know what you're doing with it.

"We are a very long way from that point. You have a lot of work to do."

I can see their shoulders sagging. The despair kicking in.

"Dismissed!"

And they slouch off to the dining room like injured puppies.

*****

I left school when I turned 16, as soon as they'd let me out of the doors. I went straight to the indoor market and found a job, cleaning and doing the filthiest tasks at the butcher's shop. Ken, the butcher, told me I wouldn't last a day. All the other girls he'd hired walked out after an hour. But I'm not other girls.

After a month of mopping blood and breaking bones and scooping chicken guts into bags, I demanded a pay rise. He was so shocked, he agreed – but it wasn't enough to leave home. Dad still thought I was at school. Where he thought I was going at five in the morning is anyone's guess. He probably never noticed.

I worked, all the days I could. After work, I ran. I had a circuit of the park I could do in the dark, in the rain, in the snow, and it kept me sane. I'd end the run with a takeaway on a park bench with the other school drop-outs, and when I went home to get some sleep I'd leave them there, drinking cheap lager and picking fights.

I got into a few fights to start with, with boys who thought they could take advantage, and girls who didn't like how I was keeping myself fit and holding down a job. We'd wind each other up, but most of the time we'd laugh it off, play-fight, and see who could swear the loudest to shock the passers-by. It was good to let go, and let off steam occasionally, but I would always be at work on time the next day. No point letting Ken down and losing my job.

The others seemed happy with this life. No ambition. No running, either. Most of them couldn't run for the bus, let alone keep up with me on a lap of the park. And I'd creep home at night, and hope that Dad was out, or already drunk enough not to care where I'd been. I'd had 16 years of practice, avoiding his shouting and his fists, but every night was a gamble. He could still hurt me if he wanted to.

I paid the rent, and kept us in the house. Who he thought was paying it, I don't know. Maybe he assumed he'd paid it himself.

And then the bombings got worse, and the government advertised for new soldiers. Good pay, proper training, and a chance at a real career. Plus they didn't care what exams you'd passed – they just wanted volun-

teers to fight their war. On my 18th birthday, I quit my job and signed up.

Ken nearly cried. He'd got used to me turning up and doing everything he asked me to do, every working day for two years. He kept saying that he wouldn't be able to find another helper like me, and asking what he was supposed to do now. I told him about the dropouts and their takeaways, and sent him to the park bench to find someone new. I don't know who got my job, but good luck to them.

I made the mistake of telling Dad I was leaving. I've never seen him so angry, and so afraid. We shouted and screamed at each other – 18 years of resentment and failure makes for a good fight. When he threatened me with a kitchen knife, I locked myself in my room and methodically packed my bag. I could hear him shouting and raging downstairs, but I knew how to stay calm, and concentrate on making sure I could carry everything I would need.

When I came downstairs to leave, he'd dropped the knife. He was sitting at the kitchen table, his head in his hands, weeping like a small child.

He begged me not go. He called me his 'little girl'. He said sorry, more times that I could count.

It wasn't enough. I walked out, caught the bus, and never looked back.

The Battle Ground series

The Battle Ground series is set in a dystopian near-future UK, after Brexit and Scottish independence.

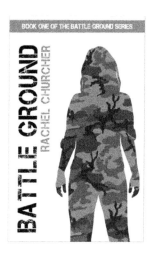

Book 1: Battle Ground

Sixteen-year-old Bex Ellman has been drafted into an army she doesn't support and a cause she doesn't believe in. Her plan is to keep her head down, and keep herself and her friends safe – until she witnesses an atrocity that she can't ignore, and a government conspiracy that threatens lives all over the UK. With her loyalties challenged, Bex must decide who to fight for – and who to leave behind.

Book 2: False Flag

Ketty Smith is an instructor with the Recruit Training Service, turning sixteen-year-old conscripts into government fighters. She's determined to win the job of lead instructor at Camp Bishop, but the arrival of Bex and her friends brings challenges she's not ready to handle. Running from her own traumatic past, Ketty faces a choice: to make a stand, and expose a government conspiracy, or keep herself safe, and hope she's working for the winning side.

Book 3: Darkest Hour

Bex Ellman and Ketty Smith are fighting on opposite sides in a British civil war. Bex and her friends are in hiding, but when Ketty threatens her family, Bex learns that her safety is more fragile than she thought.

Book 4: Fighting Back

Bex Ellman and her friends are in hiding, sheltered by the resistance. With her family threatened and her friendships challenged, she's looking for a way to fight back. Ketty Smith is in London, supporting a government she no longer trusts. With her support network crumbling, Ketty must decide who she is fighting for – and what she is willing risk to uncover the truth.

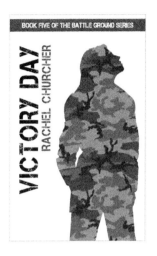

Book 5: Victory Day

Bex Ellman and Ketty Smith meet in London. As the war heats up around them, Bex and Ketty must learn to trust each other. With her friends and family in danger, Bex needs Ketty to help rescue them. For Ketty, working with Bex is a matter of survival. When Victory is declared, both will be held accountable for their decisions.

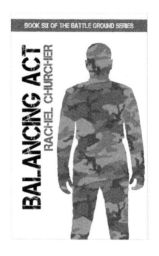

Book 6: Balancing Act

Corporal David Conrad has life figured out. His job gives him power, control, and access to Top Secret operations. His looks have tempted plenty of women into his bed, and he has no intention of committing to a relationship.

When Ketty Smith joins the Home Forces, Conrad sets his sights on the new girl – but pursuing Ketty will be more dangerous than he realises. Is Conrad about to meet his match? And will the temptations of his job distract him from his target?

Balancing Act revisits the events of *Darkest Hour*, *Fighting Back*, and *Victory Day*. **The story is suitable for older teens.**

Book 7: Finding Fire and Other Stories

What happened between Margie and Dan at Make-peace Farm? How did Jackson really feel about Ketty? What happens next to the survivors of the Battle Ground Series?

Step behind the scenes of the series with six new short stories and five new narrators – Margie, Jackson, Maz, Dan, and Charlie – plus bonus blogs and insights from the author.

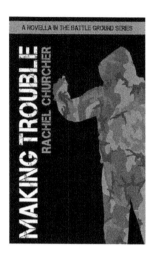

Novella: Making Trouble

Fifteen-year-old Topher Mackenzie has a complicated life. His Mum is in Australia, his Dad is struggling to look after him, and Auntie Charlie is the only person who understands. When his girlfriend is forced to leave the UK after a racist attack, Topher faces a choice: accept the government's lies, or find a way to fight back.

Download FREE from freebook.tallerbooks.com

Acknowledgements

The Battle Ground series represents more than a year of hard work – not just for me, but for the people who have supported me and helped to make it happen.

A huge thank you is due to my amazing proofreaders, who have given up their time to read every book and send me helpful and insightful feedback. Thank you to Alan Platt, Holly Platt Wells, Reba Sigler, Joe Silber, and Reynard Spiess.

Thank you to my *Battle Ground* beta readers, Jasmine Bruce, James Keen, Karen MacLaughlin, Matt Paley, and Bea Purser-Hallard for encouragement and insightful comments.

Thank you to all the people who have given me advice on the road to publication: Tim Dedopulos, Salomé Jones, Rob Manser, John Pettigrew, Danielle Zigner, and Jericho Writers.

Thank you to everyone at NaNoWriMo, for giving me the opportunity and the tools to start writing, and to everyone at YALC for inspiration and advice.

Thank you to my amazing designer, Medina Karic, for deciphering my sketches and notes and turning them into beautiful book covers. If you ever need a designer, find her at www.fiverr.com/milandra.

Thank you to Alan Platt, for learning the hard way how to live with a writer, and for bringing your start-up expertise to the creation of Taller Books.

Thank you to Alex Bate, Janina Ander, and Helen Lynn, for encouraging me to write *Battle Ground* when I suddenly had time on my hands, and for introducing me to Prosecco Fridays. Cheers!

Thank you to Hannah Pollard and the Book Club Galz for sharing so many wonderful YA books with me – and for understanding that the book is *always* better than the film.

Special mention goes to the Peatbog Faeries, whose album *Faerie Stories* is the ultimate cure for writer's block. The soundtrack to *The Greatest Showman*, and Lady Antebellum's *Need You Now*, are my go-to albums for waking up and feeling energised to write, even on the hardest days.

This book is dedicated to my family. Don't worry – I won't make you read it!

About the Author

Rachel Churcher was born between the last manned moon landing, and the first orbital Space Shuttle mission. She remembers watching the launch of STS-1, and falling in love with space flight, at the age of five. She fell in love with science fiction shortly after that, and in her teens she discovered dystopian fiction. In an effort to find out what she wanted to do with her life, she collected degrees and other qualifications in Geography, Science Fiction Studies, Architectural Technology, Childminding, and Writing for Radio.

She has worked as an editor on national and in-house magazines; as an IT trainer; and as a freelance writer and artist. She has renovated several properties, and has plenty of horror stories to tell about dangerous electrics and nightmare plumbers. She enjoys reading, travelling, stargazing, and eating good food with good friends – but nothing makes her as happy as writing fiction.

Her first published short story appeared in an anthology in 2014, and the Battle Ground series is her first long-form work. Rachel lives in East Anglia, in a house with a large library and a conservatory full of house plants. She would love to live on Mars, but only if she's allowed to bring her books.

Follow **RachelChurcherWriting** on Instagram and GoodReads.

Printed in Great Britain
by Amazon